"DO YOU KNOW WHAT I WANTED TO DO this afternoon when I saw you sitting on those rocks in the middle of nowhere?"

She saw the hungry gleam that leaped into his eyes. "You wanted to throw me off the mountain?"

"Wrong. Two more guesses."

She knew where this was heading, but she tried to prevent the inevitable. "You wanted to strangle me?"

"Last try," he said, his fingers lightly stroking her throat. She had been breathtaking sitting outside in the fading afternoon light. It had taken all his willpower not to gather her into his arms and satisfy the desire that flared every time they were together.

Tennie trembled as his touch seared her skin. The flames dancing from his fingertips matched the ones in his eyes. "You wanted to kiss me?"

He groaned and closed the distance between them. His breath softly fluttered against her mouth. "More than that, Tennie. I wanted to lay you down on a bed of soft pine needles and lose myself in you so far it'd be a week before I found my way back. . . ."

WHAT ARE *LOVESWEPT* ROMANCES?

They are stories of true romance and touching emotion. We believe those two very important ingredients are constants in our highly sensual and very believable stories in the LOVESWEPT line. Our goal is to give you, the reader, stories of consistently high quality that may sometimes make you laugh, sometimes make you cry, but are always fresh and creative and contain many delightful surprises within their pages.

Most romance fans read an enormous number of books. Those they truly love, they keep. Others may be traded with friends and soon forgotten. We hope that each LOVESWEPT romance will be a treasure—a "keeper." We will always try to publish

LOVE STORIES YOU'LL NEVER FORGET BY AUTHORS YOU'LL ALWAYS REMEMBER

The Editors

Loveswept ® 687

PLAYING FOR KEEPS

MARCIA EVANICK

BANTAM BOOKS

NEW YORK · TORONTO · LONDON · SYDNEY · AUCKLAND

PLAYING FOR KEEPS

A Bantam Book / May 1994

*If you would be interested in receiving protective vinyl covers for your
Loveswept books, please write to this address for information:*

Loveswept
Bantam Books
P.O. Box 985
Hicksville, NY 11802

ISBN 0-553-44328-3

Published simultaneously in the United States and Canada

Bantam Books are published by Bantam Books, a division of Bantam Dou-
bleday Dell Publishing Group, Inc. Its trademark, consisting of the words
"Bantam Books" and the portrayal of a rooster, is Registered in U.S. Patent
and Trademark Office and in other countries. Marca Registrada. Bantam
Books, 1540 Broadway, New York, New York 10036.

PRINTED IN THE UNITED STATES OF AMERICA

OPM   0 9 8 7 6 5 4 3 2 1

To Nita,
Because you believed from
the very beginning. Thanks.

PROLOGUE

The smell of death is in the air. Beware!

Tennie Montgomery's fingers trembled with excitement as she read the warning on the printed card for the third time. Her great-aunt Georgia really had gone all out this year. The blood-soaked dagger added a nice "homey" touch, and Tennie particularly loved the way the spilled blood had been smeared into forming the word, "Beware." No return address, no time, no date. Hell, they didn't even bother to print the location this year. Montgomery family reunions were unique in every way—including mayhem, murder, and a touch of madness. Tennie loved getting together with her family and solving the annual mystery—or she had until two years ago when *he'd* shown up.

She glanced around her office and frowned. Three plants sat on top of the radiator, turning into kindling, and the venetian blinds were still hanging on a drunken diagonal. Mounds of folders, papers, VCR equipment, and books overflowed every surface in the room. She pushed aside three days' worth of coffee cups and candy bar wrappers and plopped her feet up on top of her desk. Junk mail, surveillance photos, and a stack of bills went sliding off the desk.

She stared at the hole worn in the toe of her sneaker and the fuchsia-colored sock peeking through. It was time! She had been eagerly waiting ten months for this day, and the taste of revenge was sweet on her lips as she smiled, turning her head toward the door. Completely ignoring the intercom buried somewhere on her desk, she shouted, "Clair?"

"Yeah," came bellowing back from the outer office.

"Clear my calendar."

There was a distinct groan from beyond the door. Tennie grinned. Clair had been her secretary and right hand for the past five years and knew the routine by now. The Tennessee Montgomery Detective Agency wouldn't survive a month without Clair who was now reminding her, "You have the Bingingham's case coming up in court next week."

Tennie's smile never faltered as Clair came and stood in the doorway. She was on the plus side of plump and had a warm motherly outlook on life. Clair had never met a criminal who couldn't be reformed or a child who didn't need love.

"Get Hank to take over the Bingingham case," Tennie said.

Clair looked down at the appointment book in her hand and sighed. "When are you leaving?"

"Invitation doesn't say." Tennie stuck her finger into a half-filled coffee cup and frowned. It was ice cold.

"Where is it this year?"

"Doesn't say." Tennie finger-tested two more cups.

Clair grimaced, walked over to the desk, and started to remove the cups Tennie had tested.

Tennie smiled as her finger flicked the liquid in the sixth cup. "Found it." She picked up the cup and drank the remaining lukewarm coffee.

"There's a fresh pot sitting right through that door."

"Too much to do." She swept her arms through the air indicating the mounds of paper piled on the desk.

Clair snorted, lifted up one of Tennie's feet, and plucked the letter she had just typed from the pile. "You're out for blood this year, aren't you?" She absently wiped at the dirt streak on the paper and continued to stare at her employer.

"*He* won the last two years." Tennie lowered her feet and stood up. Just thinking of *that* man made her blood pressure soar. "This year it's my turn." She stalked over to the window and stared out. Jeff MacPherson's old pickup truck backfired twice as it slowly made its way down Main Street. "*He* thinks I'm some hick detective. Strictly small town."

"Aren't you?" Clair hid her smile as she busily cleaned up the rest of the coffee cups and candy wrappers.

"Just because I prefer living in the country doesn't make me a hick." She stalked back over to the desk and waved a swanky women's catalog at Clair. "This year I'll show him who's a hick."

"Aren't you going a bit overboard? Why be so concerned about your cousin?"

"Reece Carpenter is no more my cousin than the man in the moon," Tennie shouted. "Just because Uncle Utah married his mother three years ago, doesn't give him the right to barge into our family reunions and solve the mysteries."

"You're just jealous because you were winning every year until he came along to steal some of your glory."

"Am not jealous." Tennie pouted. "I can lose and with good grace." She rummaged through the papers on her desk looking for chocolate. She found a candy bar stuck in her pencil holder and shook it at Clair. "*That* man just doesn't belong there."

"Tennessee Ellery Montgomery," Clair said, chuckling on the way to the door. "I think you're protesting too much."

ONE

Tennie fought her way out of the cocoon of blankets twisted around her and reached for the shrilling phone. The illuminated red digits of her clock pierced the dark. Four-thirty in the morning was an ungodly hour for anyone to be calling. " 'Lo?"

"Tennie, dear, is that you?"

"Aunt Maine?" Tennie sat up and flipped on the bedside light.

"It's just terrible, dear," sobbed her aunt, "just terrible."

"What's terrible?"

"They arrested Uncle Colorado and won't let us see him."

Alarmed, Tennie asked, "Arrested him for what?"

"Murder, dear, murder."

Tennie relaxed. The family reunion had begun. "Who did he kill?"

"He didn't kill anyone," Aunt Maine cried.

"Then who was murdered?" Tennie grabbed a pen and a half-read detective thriller off the nightstand and started taking notes.

"Some mechanic named Taylor Taylor."

"Taylor Taylor?"

"I know it's a strange name, but wait until you hear his nickname."

"What's that?"

"Tailpipe."

Tennie bit the plastic top of her pen to keep from commenting on the choice of this year's name. "How did Mr. Tailpipe meet his demise?"

" '84 Ford pickup truck."

"Hit-and-run?"

"Nope, smashed him flatter than a floppy disk."

"What do you mean, smashed him?"

"He was working on the pickup in his shop when the hydraulic lift thing malfunctioned and dropped the truck faster than you could say pancake."

"Well, if the hydraulic lift malfunctioned, who's calling it murder?"

"The local yokels in all their lofty powers said the lift was tampered with."

"So why arrest Uncle Colorado?"

"Turns out Uncle Colorado was playing more than a game of footsie with the grieving widow, Emma Sue."

Tennie couldn't contain her chuckle. "Uncle Colorado is eighty-two years young!"

"Wait until you see Emma Sue. She's at least

seventy and bakes a cherry pie that would turn any man's head."

"Where exactly are Emma Sue, Uncle Colorado, the local yokels, and the crushed Tailpipe?" So far none of the Montgomery family reunions had been held in the same state twice. Since the day she was born, Tennie had traveled from ocean to ocean for these quaint little get-togethers with her family. This year she was praying for Hawaii. She wanted to work on her tan.

"In a town called Little Lincoln, Nevada."

"Where's that?"

"About forty miles south of Carson City. It's snuggled in the Sierras. Wait till you see it, Tennie. It's so beautiful now. Spring is Little Lincoln's best season."

Tennie sighed. So much for the tan. "Okay, Aunt Maine, give me the name of the hotel."

"It's not a hotel, dear, it's a rustic inn called The Grizzly's Revenge. There are stuffed animals on the walls, nature trails, and fishing."

Tennie only half listened as Maine went on about the inn. She glanced across her bedroom at the half dozen brand-new clingy and sophisticated dresses hanging on her closet door and sighed.

Reece Carpenter nursed his bourbon, gazed around the room, and frowned. The lounge area was packed with all of his recently acquired relatives waiting for the briefing to begin. All except one, his nemesis, his rival, his cousin-by-marriage, Tennessee Ellery Montgomery. Not only was she a thorn in his side, but she was the reason behind the ache in his loins. It had been ten months since he had last seen her and he hadn't had a good night's sleep since. He compared every woman he dated to Tennie and his dates always came up holding the short straw. Tennie had a way about her that simultaneously frustrated and excited him. She was intelligent, beautiful, and knew more about the detective business than Sherlock Holmes. She also had the most kissable mouth he had ever seen.

Three years ago, while he was out of town on a case, his mother had called in the legendary detective Utah Montgomery to investigate the disappearance of artifacts from the museum where she was working. Three months later the artifacts were recovered and Reece ended up with a stepfather who dominated his own profession.

Just when he was beginning to feel secure with Utah, he was invited to the Montgomerys' family reunion. The name Montgomery could be traced back to the early Pinkerton days when two of the agency's best detectives fell in love and started a dynasty of their own. Needing to prove the name Carpenter was as good as Montgomery, Reece had pulled out every stop and solved The Mystery of the Poisoned Priest. He had won the admiration and respect of every Montgomery except one—Tennie.

Last year when the reunion was held in Hollywood and a mythical producer bit the dust, Reece had tried to be more friendly with Tennie. When she wasn't swaying her cute little tush or laughing her throaty laugh, she was beating him to every clue. All-out war had been declared between them, privately of course, and with a stroke of luck on his side he had uncovered the final clue and solved the mystery a mere four minutes before her. The entire Montgomery clan had enjoyed the private show more than the actual mystery. He had gone looking for Tennie after everything had calmed down only to discover she had hopped the first plane back to Iowa and out of his life.

The bourbon in Reece's glass started to spill as Florida Montgomery's voice carried through the room. "Did you see Tennie? My God, what did she do to herself?"

He strained his ears but couldn't pick up the reply. *What was wrong with Tennie?* He knew she had checked in about two hours before, but so far he hadn't spotted her. He looked around the room again trying to see her golden ponytail or her jean-clad bottom. Reece's gaze slipped over questioning glances cast his way from his mother and Utah. The Montgomerys could pick up the slightest emotion and he was afraid Utah had zeroed in on his fascination with Tennie.

Reece took a sip of bourbon and silently studied the two local police officers. He had been spending so much of his time concentrating on Tennie that he hadn't paid much attention to the mystery that was unfolding around him. Vital clues had been dropped, leaked, or concealed during the past fifteen minutes, and he hadn't picked up on a one. The problem with the Montgomerys' reunions was that nothing was as it seemed. The two officers could be the entire force of Little Lincoln, as they claimed, or they could be actors. The Montgomerys were notorious for stacking the town with actors who lied, dropped false clues, and generally muddied the entire investigation. Just like real life. The elder Montgomerys, who were retired, had nothing better to do than to plan these mysteries, sit back, and watch the rest of the family stumble around making complete fools of themselves until the mystery was solved. Reece couldn't wait until he retired.

A momentary silence fell over the group, and Reece knew without glancing toward the door that Tennie had arrived. He slowly turned his gaze away from the two officers and toward the beautiful woman graciously making her way into the room. Aunt Florida was right! What has Tennie been up to these past ten months? Where were the jeans, the beaten-up sneakers, or the sassy ponytail that made her look like a twenty-year-old college student instead of the twenty-eight-year-old professional she was?

His gaze slid down the silky coral-colored dress that accented every one of Tennie's curves as she made her way across the room toward her grandmother Ada, affectionately known to the family as Grandmom Pinky. The two previous reunions had shown him one thing about Tennie, she doted on the old woman. Not that he blamed her. Grandmom Pinky was a spry old lady somewhere in her late seventies who was usually the mastermind behind these reunions. Her nickname came, of course, from the Pinkerton Detective Agency.

Tonight Grandmom Pinky didn't look so spry. In fact she looked frail and ashen. Reece noticed the concern on Tennie's face as she sat down next to the old woman and took her thin trembling hand. He tried to concentrate on reading Tennie's lips as she whispered to her grandmother. But the more he watched those lush lips, the more uncomfortable he became. He downed the rest of his bourbon, tried to ignore the heat suffusing his body, and tuned out the report of Tailpipe's murder being given by the two officers.

Tennie nervously smoothed a wrinkle on her skirt and recrossed her legs. She knew she had caused a small sensation when she had walked into the room. None of her family had been prepared for the new Tennie. While everyone was thrown off balance by her sudden change in appearance, she was going to solve the mystery. At least that had been her game plan before she'd entered the lounge and encountered Reece's devastating stare. Now she was lucky if she'd remember where she was, let alone the blubbering of the two officers going on about autopsy reports, cause of death, the mechanics of a hydraulic lift, and motive. If Reece didn't stop staring, she either was going to scream or melt into a steaming puddle of need. He

was the most virile man she had ever laid eyes on—
and the most aggravating.

Two years ago, when she first met him, she nearly
had drooled during the introduction. She had spent
the entire reunion in a daze and had managed to
muff the investigation so badly, that Reece had ended
up winning. It had been a painful lesson on how
personal feelings could screw up a case. Last year
she had been bound and determined to control the
attraction she felt for Reece and beat him. Within
twenty-four hours of their meeting, she and he had
declared war, and the battle of the sleuths had started.
Reece obviously hadn't felt any of the attraction that
assaulted her during their time together. Once during
the investigation they were alone by themselves in a
dark, secluded basement, chasing down a clue. She
thought it had been the perfect place for a stolen kiss.
Reece ended up stealing the clue and locking her in. It
had taken her a little over seven minutes to beat down
the door and months to repair her wounded pride. She
wasn't about to make that mistake again. This year it
was going to be totally different.

"Tennie, sweetheart?"

She came out of her daze and flushed when she
realized her grandfather was standing in front of her.
"I'm sorry, Granddad, did you say something?"

"I need to see you in private for a minute." Indiana
Montgomery picked up his wife's hand and gallantly
placed a kiss on her knuckles. "If you would excuse us
for a few minutes, dear."

"Of course, Indy." Grandmom Pinky patted Tennie on the knee. "Run along, child."

Tennie brushed a kiss across her grandmother's cheek and followed her grandfather out of the lounge, across the reception area of the inn, and into what appeared to be a private reading room or office. A fire blazed merrily in the fireplace and rich deep green leather chairs formed a semicircle around its glow. Huge tree-size plants complimented overflowing bookshelves and glass-enclosed Indian artifacts begging to be admired. Tennie would have felt more at ease if there weren't at least a dozen stuffed animal heads staring glassy-eyed down at her, and if her grandfather weren't standing at the door, frowning.

She squashed the urge to lean against the mantel and warm herself by the fire. Nylons, a satin slip, and delicate lacy undies were no protection for the chilly evenings of a Sierra spring. Being a lady of fashion could be hazardous to one's health. Tennie sat down in the chair closest to the flames and crossed her legs. "You wanted to see me, Grandfather?"

Indiana Montgomery's frown changed into a smile. "There you are, son, I thought you might have forgotten."

Tennie glanced over her shoulder and groaned. Reece Carpenter stood in the doorway looking incredibly handsome, entirely in control, and worst of all, warm. His concession to roughing it in the Sierras was a sport coat, no tie, and cotton twill pants. "You told me to make it look casual, sir."

"So I did, Reece. Thanks. Please come in and close the door."

"Make what look casual?" Tennie asked.

Reece closed the door and took the chair directly opposite her. Long luscious legs shimmering in the firelight caught his imagination. "Following him and you in here." He pulled his gaze and thoughts away from the seductive trap of pondering what it would feel like to have her wrap those scrumptious legs around his waist. He turned his attention to the elderly man sitting between them. "You wanted to see us, sir?"

"Indy, Reece. Please call me Indy." He felt in his pockets for a pack of cigarettes, momentarily forgetting he had given up the habit fifteen years ago.

Tennie noticed the slip and frowned. Grandfather Indy never slipped. "What's wrong?"

He leaned forward and gently patted her hand. "Now, now, Tennie, you mustn't worry so."

She visibly paled and clutched at his hand. "Pop-Pop, tell me what's wrong."

"It's been years since you called me that." He wiped at a sentimental tear clouding his vision and sighed. "It's Pinky."

"Grandmom?"

"Unless you know of another Pinky roaming the earth, and then all I can say is God help us all." His gaze turned thoughtful as he studied the flames in the hearth.

Tennie glanced from her grandfather to Reece,

who silently shrugged his shoulders, and back again. "Grandfather, what's wrong with Grandmom?"

He continued to stare into the flames. "It's her heart, Tennie. They tell me the thing I love most about that woman is old and weak."

"Who told you?"

"Doctors, specialists. More doctors." He clutched his trembling fingers together. "For the past six months she has seen more doctors and had more tests than in her entire life. Sixty years of married life and five children later and there's nothing I can do but pray."

Utterly speechless, Tennie stared at her grandfather. Reece jumped to his feet and started to pace. Grandmom Pinky had come to mean a great deal to him over the last couple of years. "There's got to be something we can do."

"That's why I called you two in here," Indy said.

Reece and Tennie quickly glanced at each other and eagerly said, "What?"

Indy studied the worried young man standing in front of the mantel. "Reece, do you realize how important you and your mother have become to this family?" Without waiting for an answer he continued, "Pinky and I had given up the hope of Utah ever finding someone special. From the day he married your mom we have looked on you as another grandson."

"Thank you, sir."

"No thanks needed, son." Indy turned his attention to Tennie. "You, young lady, have always been special to us. You're the youngest of the grandchildren and something of a rebel. Not a day goes by without Pinky worrying about you."

"Granddad, there's no need for you or Grandmom to worry. I can take care of myself." She brushed an imaginary piece of lint off her skirt. She didn't like the idea of her grandparents worrying about her.

"I know that, honey, but Pinky's a little hard to convince. She still has some of the old-fashioned rules embedded in her very liberal head." He glanced at Reece and smiled. "Pinky's convinced Tennie will never snag herself a husband because she can't cook."

"Grandfather!"

Reece grinned.

"A man can't live by bread alone." Indy winked at Reece. "Can he, son?"

Reece winked back. "Not to my knowledge, sir."

"If a man's hungry, he should go to a restaurant, right, son?"

"Yes, sir."

Indy ignored his granddaughter's indignant glare. "If a man wants a clean home, he should hire a maid, right, son?"

Reece leaned against the mantel and relaxed. "I find it's cheaper that way, sir."

Indy burst out laughing and slapped his leg. "Damn, son, that was a good one. There's only one reason for someone to get married. The same reason I married my darling Pinky sixty years ago."

"Love, sir?"

"There was that, son, but the main reason was I couldn't keep my hands off her." Both men chuckled knowingly.

Tennie's fingers gripped the arm of the chair. "If you two are done swapping helpful hints for chauvinists, I would like to get back to the issue of my grandmother's health."

Reece and Indy sobered immediately. "I'm sorry, child," said Indy. "Everything that can be done for Pinky is being done, but there is one small favor I want from you and Reece."

"What's that?"

"I want you two to behave yourselves this year."

Tennie glared at Reece and he cocked an eyebrow. "Grandfather," Tennie questioned, "when haven't we behaved ourselves?"

"Last year the entire reunion turned into a guessing game. Everyone was so caught up watching you two trying to outwit each other that no one was following the clues to the murder. Pinky spent months helping to plan that crime and no one gave it any real justice except you two." He leveled a serious stare at Tennie and Reece. "For the last ten months Pinky has been meticulously going over every detail of this reunion, and I don't want her being upset again."

Tennie swallowed hard. "Again?"

"Last year she wasn't really happy the way you disabled Reece's car, Tennie. Reece is family now and should be treated as such." He ignored the fiery flush sweeping his granddaughter's cheeks and turned to

Reece. "And you, son, should be ashamed of yourself for locking a defenseless young woman in that basement so you could follow up on some clue."

Reece felt like a heel now, but at the time it seemed like a good idea. The temptation to haul her into his arms and kiss her until she went up in flames had been too real. He had practically tasted that kiss just by gazing at her mouth. He had wanted her more than he had wanted to solve the mystery and that had scared him. He'd had to get out of that dark, seductive basement in a hurry or he was going to follow up on every one of his fantasies with his stepfather's goddaughter. The more space he put between them, the better off he would be. "Tennie's not defenseless, sir. She was out of there in ten minutes."

"Seven minutes and twenty-four seconds." Tennie smiled sweetly at Reece. "But who's counting?"

Reece nodded. "Next time I'll make sure there aren't any heavy instruments laying around before I lock the door."

"See! That's exactly what I mean. You two haven't even been in the same room for ten minutes and already you're fighting." Indy slowly got to his feet and warmed his hands in front of the fire. "Pinky wants this reunion to be the best one ever, and by golly I will make sure it is. I want you two to put aside your differences and work together on this case."

"Together?" Tennie and Reece cried in unison.

"Yes, together," Indy said. "It is Pinky's deepest desire to see you two get along, and you will even if I have to hog-tie you two together until the mystery is solved." He briskly rubbed his hands. "Are there any questions?"

"Can't we just be friends," implored Tennie.

"How can you be friends when you're out there trying to outwit each other? The only way is for you two to work together in solving the murder." Indy calmly regarded his granddaughter's rebellious glare. "Not for me, Tennie, but for Pinky. Do it for Pinky. It might be her last reunion."

Tennie sighed in defeat. How could she possibly refuse? "I agree, if he does."

"*He* has a name, and it's Reece." Reece turned his attention to Indy. "I will be more than honored to do this one small favor for Pinky. She has come to mean a great deal to me these past couple of years, sir."

Indy graciously nodded his head. "I thank you both. I'm sure if you get to know each other you will realize how much you have in common." He glanced at his watch. "Now, if you will excuse me, it's time for Pinky's pill." He was halfway out the door when he turned and said, "By the way, if you want to win, you had better get on the ball. I noticed at least three clues had been dropped that neither of you seemed to pick up on." He sadly shook his head, turned around, and headed back into the lounge packed with Montgomerys, police, waiters, and actors.

Reece glanced over at Tennie who was staring into the fire, and he groaned. This was never going to work. Her grandfather was right. They couldn't spend ten minutes in the same room without arguing. He knew why he argued with Tennie constantly—it diverted all his senses away from the real problem. He wanted Tennessee Montgomery. He wanted to lay her down on the intricately handwoven rug in front of the fire and sink himself so deep within her, he wouldn't be able to come up for air for a week. He wanted the legendary Indiana Montgomery's granddaughter beneath him, naked, and wildly screaming his name in ecstasy. He uttered an oath at his body's reaction and turned his back on Tennie. Reece jammed his hands into his pockets and glared at the mounted head of a poor bighorn sheep.

"I'm sorry, did you say something?" Tennie asked.

He continued to study the animal. "I said, how about if I make up some emergency back at my office and head on out of here?"

"Don't you dare!" Tennie jumped to her feet and moved closer to the fire. Damn it was cold. "If you leave now, they will think it's all my fault. Grandfather would probably disinherit me."

"Is the inheritance that important to you?" He really couldn't say he knew Tennie well, but he had always been a pretty good judge of character. She didn't strike him as the materialistic type.

Startled, Tennie looked up. "It was only a figure of speech. I do not want, or expect anything from my grandparents, or my parents either." She bristled. "I have to join my aunt Florida for dinner." She took a step toward the door. "So, please excuse me."

"Tennie, wait. I'm sorry. I didn't mean anything by that." He swallowed hard at the way the flames dancing behind her silhouetted her flawless legs through the silky thinness of her dress.

She studied his expression. He truly was sorry. It wasn't his fault she had this thing about being a Montgomery. All her life people automatically assumed she was getting a free ride off Indy's famous coattails, either financially or by cases being passed her way. She had worked for years building her own reputation in a small corner of Iowa without a Montgomery within five hundred miles. With that one harmless question, Reece had brought back all the old doubt and hurt. "Apology accepted." She turned once again toward the door. "Now, if you will excuse me, I really have to go."

"But what about the case and the clues we already missed? Shouldn't we be discussing it?"

"Not tonight, Reece. I have other plans." She absently played with the gold clasp of her bracelet. "I'll keep my eyes and ears open tonight and tomorrow we'll compare notes over breakfast. How does that sound?"

"Seven all right with you?"

Tennie groaned. "How about nine?"

Reece chuckled. "I forgot you're not a morning person."

She felt a flush sweep up her cheeks at the memory of how he knew she wasn't a morning person. Last year at their swank Hollywood hotel one of her charming teenage cousins decided to play bongo drums on her door at six-thirty in the morning. Reece had just come out of his room as she threw open her door and proceeded to rip into the boy. Hollywood would have given the scene an "R" rating.

Reece's gaze involuntarily dropped to her luscious legs. He remembered every detail from that morning. He couldn't recall what was shouted, or even which cousin she had been ripping into, but he remembered her legs. Tennie had dashed out of her room, wearing nothing but a white T-shirt with a ridiculous eyeball printed on the front. With each motion of her arms and every breath she took, the shirt rode higher up her thighs. He had been in the process of having heart failure when she had noticed him, snapped a few last words at the boy, and slammed back into her room. He had been less than an inch away from discovering if her hair was naturally golden blond.

"How about if we compromise? Eight o'clock?" He forced his gaze away from her legs and his mind back into the present.

"Fine, just don't expect me to be fully awake and have the coffee waiting." She walked out the door, calling over her shoulder, "And remember, I do my best work at night."

Reece sank his teeth into the tender part of his hand beneath his thumb to keep himself from saying any one of the wicked things that popped into his mind.

TWO

Tennie climbed the stairs feeling drained, even if it was only a little after midnight. The anxiety of finding out her grandmother was ill coupled with having to work with Reece until the mystery was solved had hit her hard. Maybe she should invent some emergency back at her office and let Reece take the heat for running her off. Only problem was that she had never run from anything in her life and she wasn't about to start now. When she left the security of her family five years ago to start her own business, she hadn't been running away from something, she had been running to something. A new beginning. She was either going to make it on her own, or not. She had made it. Working with Reece for the next couple of days, she wasn't sure she was going to make it.

The man inspired intense emotions better left unexplored and cloaked with indifferent or politeness. She was never indifferent to Reece and polite would be stretching the truth by yards. How was she going to keep these unwanted feelings hidden if she had to spend hours every day in his company?

She reached the second floor landing, kicked off her high heels, and rubbed her aching toes. Who had she been trying to impress with the fancy hairstyle, sophisticated dress, and three-inch killer heels? Reece that was who! The person who had seemed most impressed was one of the local cops who'd maneuvered her into a corner after dinner and tried putting the make on her. She had allowed herself to be monopolized so she could pump him for information about the case. She had been ninety percent sure the playboy cop was an actor planted by her family when Reece's thunderous glare from across the room caught her eye. Who did he think he was? Reece might be her unwanted partner, but he wasn't going to be her keeper. She had returned his glare with a sweet smile and continued to grill the cop.

Tennie inserted the key and opened the door to her room. Moonlight poured through the balcony doors and bathed the room in a soft glow. She closed the door behind her; with a deep sigh she tossed the torturous shoes into the farthest corner. Her suitcase still lay open with half its contents flung over the bed, the chair, and the small counter in the bathroom. It was amazing that the other five brand-new outfits that she had recently purchased had found their way onto hangers, if not into the closet. Neatness was not one of the top priorities in her life.

Weary, she tossed her small clutch purse onto the pile of shimmering undies scattered across the bed and, without bothering to turn on any lights, yanked the hem of her dress to midthigh. Her fingers made short work of the two garter snaps and bracing her foot on the bed she started to roll the silky nylons down her leg.

"Have you ever given any thought to declaring those legs as lethal weapons?"

Tennie's startled gaze shot to her purse where a can of Mace rested secure and unreachable within its depths. As her heart started to beat again she realized it had been Reece's voice she heard. Refusing to be intimidated or embarrassed she slowly turned her head in the direction from which his voice had materialized. Her fingers continued to roll the nylons down over her calf and off her foot. "My tae kwon do instructor told me it wasn't necessary"—she smiled sweetly—"yet."

Reece chuckled and flipped the switch next to his hand, flooding the room with light. He leaned against the jamb of the interconnecting door and continued to gaze hungrily at her legs. "I wasn't referring to kicking someone to death."

Tennie slowly lowered her leg and smoothed the dress back down. The other stocking could wait until later. She didn't like the direction the conversation was heading. "Do you always stand around in the dark sulking?" She flipped on the bedside light.

"I wasn't sulking." He walked into the room and glanced around.

"Then what were you doing standing in the dark, spying on me?" She cocked her head and studied him from the new angle. He was so handsome, and his thick black hair cried out for a woman's touch. He towered over her five-feet-six-inch height by a good six inches. Ridiculously thick black lashes framed a pair of deep brown intelligent eyes that always seemed to be asking questions. What they were asking now she couldn't begin to fathom.

"I wasn't spying on you. I was waiting to see if they were coming back."

She glanced around the room perplexed. "Who was coming back?"

"The guys who did this." Reece flung his arm out to encompass the whole room. A huge canvas purse was dumped upside down on the middle of the bed, spilling its contents across the quilt and onto the floor. Tubes of lipstick, candy bars, a can of diet cola, wads of tissues, a couple of paperbacks, and a wilted corsage were just a few of the items scattered about. "You better go through everything and see what's missing."

Tennie glanced around the room in amazement. Reece thought someone had ransacked the room. Whoever heard of anyone pulling a heist in the middle of the Montgomerys' family reunion? "Reece, I wasn't robbed."

He glanced questioningly at Tennie, then back at the room. Understanding finally dawned. He stared incredulously at Tennie. "Tell me you're joking."

"I'm joking." Tennie pushed a pair of jeans off the chair and sat down. "May I ask what you were doing in my room?"

"I wasn't in your room; I was in mine." He touched the pile of clothes near the edge of the bed, realized they were Tennie's silken undies, and snatched his hand back as if they were on fire. He quickly paced to the other end of the room and looked out the balcony doors. "I returned to my room about fifteen minutes ago."

Tennie glanced at his sturdy boots, tight-fitting jeans, and his sweatshirt that hadn't had the time or washings to lose its shape yet. He looked all warm and yummy. "Where did you go?"

He glanced back over his shoulder. "For a walk." He wasn't about to tell her he left the warmth of the lodge to wander around some pine forest in the middle of the night so that he could get a grip on his emotions. He had wanted to smack the lovesick-puppy-dog look off the face of that young police officer who had cornered Tennie. When he noticed Tennie wasn't minding all the attention, he had stormed up to his room, changed, and headed for cool air and sanity. Whatever Tennie did was her own business.

"Find any clues?"

"Not a one." Tennie had the same view from her windows as his room. Miles and miles of mountains, trees, and darkness. He ignored the panoramic view of nature and concentrated on Tennie's reflection in the glass.

"Really, Reece." Tennie crossed her legs and lightly swung the nylon-covered limb back and forth. "If you're going to work with me, you are going to have to help discover some clues."

Reece's back stiffened as he slowly turned and faced her. "And what precisely did you find out tonight?"

There was such a sarcastic slur to his question that Tennie couldn't resist teasing him. "I discovered that French-cut undies weren't meant for this climate." She wondered how many cases of frostbite of the derriere the local hospital treated each year.

Reece's voice sounded like someone was strangling him. "Tennie!"

She raised one eyebrow. "You still haven't explained what you were doing spying on me."

Exasperated, he ran a hand through his hair. "I checked the connecting door to see if it was locked. It wasn't."

"So why didn't you lock it?"

"I tried, but the lock must be broken. I knocked, and when no one answered I opened the door. Not knowing what an immaculate housekeeper you are, I naturally thought the room had been ransacked. Before I could make up my mind what to do I heard your key in the door and turned out my lights to see if the thugs were coming back."

Tennie stood up and walked over to the wall unit containing the thermostat. She put it on high. "You must have made one hell of a Boy Scout, Reece."

Reece gazed at her luscious bottom and tried desperately not to think of French-cut undies. He failed miserably. "I'll call down to the front desk and have them send someone up to fix the lock."

"It's after midnight." She rubbed her hands together. "It can wait until morning." Having an unlocked door as the only barrier between Reece and herself didn't upset her. She knew more about Reece and his mother than probably Uncle Utah did. When Uncle Utah announced he met and married Celeste Carpenter, Tennie had pulled in a couple of favors and had a complete dossier on both Celeste and Reece on her desk within days. The reading had been as interesting as traffic signs on a one-way street. Both Reece and his mother could have qualified as Supreme Court justices. Not one ounce of dirt, mud, or scandal could be found anywhere.

Reece watched her hands generate warmth and thought about her frozen bottom. He jammed his hands deep into the pockets of his jeans. "Did you happen to hear any of the autopsy report?" He knew for a fact she hadn't been paying attention when the report was given. He had heard bits and pieces, but he, too, had been distracted.

"I'll have a copy of the actual report in my hands before breakfast."

"How?"

"Jake the Fake." She pulled out the remaining clothes in the enormous suitcase and tossed them on top of the bureau. With a triumphant smile she snatched up a lumpy gray sweat suit and headed for the bathroom.

"Who's Jake the Fake?"

"The young cop with the overactive hormones." She paused at the bathroom door. "If you want to continue discussing what I found out tonight, you will have to wait until I put on something warm." She just about closed the door, leaving an inch of space to talk through. "Gee, if I would have known it was going to be this cold, I would have packed my long johns."

Reece glared at the closed door. "What do you mean by *overactive hormones*?"

Tennie chuckled. "You sound like a protective big brother."

"I'm not your brother, Montana is. By the way where is he? I haven't seen him yet."

"I'm not sure if he's going to make it this year. Sue Ellen just delivered another baby boy three weeks ago. I guess it will all depend on how she and little Galveston are doing."

Reece tried to disregard the enticing rustle of silk behind the closed door. "Why's Montana breaking the Montgomery tradition of naming kids after states? Aren't all his boys named after cities in Texas?"

"Yep." Tennie's voice was muffled for a moment. Reece envisioned the sweatshirt being yanked over her head. "There's Austin, Dallas, Houston, and now little Galveston. Montana and Sue Ellen wanted to start their own tradition, and besides all the good states were taken. Montana always swore no child of his would go through life with the name of New Hampshire."

Reece chuckled. "He has a point there." He waited for the sound of running water to stop before asking, "Are you going to name your kids after states?"

Tennie opened up the door and tossed the silky dress over the back of a chair. "Haven't even thought about it." She was wearing a stretched-out, faded, entirely comfortable, warm gray sweat suit. She had scrubbed the makeup off her face and brushed out the fancy hairstyle that had taken her forty minutes to perfect. She felt more in control. More like her true self again.

"You never thought about what you would name your kids?"

"Nope, I haven't even thought about having them." She sorted through a pile of lingerie and pulled out a pair of thick teal-colored socks. She sat in the chair and put them on.

"Why not?" It had been his experience that any woman approaching thirty was at least asking herself about settling down and starting a family.

"First off I'd make a lousy single parent. My cats would starve to death if they didn't remind me to feed them once a day. Second—"

"I didn't know you had cats."

"Dick and Peter have me, I don't have them."

"Dick and Peter?" Reece couldn't prevent the lewd grin that spread across his face.

"Dick Tracy and Peter Gunn are their full names, so get your mind out of the gutter."

He tried to force the grin into a pleasant smile. "What's your second reason?"

"Mr. Right would have to be downright insane to marry me. There's one thing I do worse than keeping house."

Reece glanced around the room in horror. She was worse at something else? "What's that?"

"Cooking. If it doesn't come in its own cardboard box with microwave instructions printed on the back, it doesn't get bought."

He shuddered at the thought of eating dinner out of a cardboard box. "You may have a point there."

Tennie wiggled her toes. The feeling was coming back into them. "I don't think tracking down stolen jewelry, coming up with a motive for using some guy's head for target practice, or following a sleazeball of a husband while he cheats on his wife are the kind of qualities most men look for in a wife. Right?"

"I guess not. Most men don't consider knowing thirty-six untraceable poisons as a bonus in the marriage market."

Tennie grinned. She knew of at least thirty-eight. "Why haven't you tied the big knot yet?" She didn't like all the focus directed her way and besides that, she was curious. Reece was handsome, had a body that was built for pleasure, owned his own business, and was intelligent enough to guarantee there would be conversation over the breakfast table for the next fifty years. So why hadn't he married and produced the grandkids that Celeste and Uncle Utah had been clamoring for?

Reece looked uncomfortable for a moment. "I guess for the same reasons you haven't."

Tennie arched one brow. "You're a slob too?"

"No." He watched as that one brow shot higher. "What I mean is, I don't mind picking up after myself and cooking can be a great tension reducer." He started gently to push the scattered items spread out across the floor into a pile with the toe of his boot. "I was referring to the work we do. Most women find it exciting at first, but then the long hours, the trips out of town, and constant danger begin to wear the relationship pretty thin."

"Yeah, most murderers I've met don't want to be caught. And being stood up for dinner because of some hot lead just doesn't cut it too often."

Reece nodded. "Do tell. I once had a date jam the bouquet of roses I brought as an apology into her garbage disposal and then proceeded to hurl the thorny stems at my head."

Tennie grinned at the picture of him dodging flying stems. "That was rude of her."

"It was the third time in a row I stood her up. I guess understanding only goes so far."

"I guess so. It looks like we're both destined to be single unless some crazy or saintly person comes along." She pulled her legs up onto the chair and rested her chin on top of her knees. "You have my sincerest sympathy, Reece."

"Why?"

"At least I have Montana and Sue Ellen producing all those darling grandchildren for my parents. It keeps the heat off my back. But you're an only child."

"It's funny but my mom never worried about me being single until she met and married Utah. Now that she's experiencing marital bliss she has been hinting to me about settling down and giving her a grandchild to spoil."

A devilish smile lit Tennie's face. "I bet Utah hasn't been that meek in his opinion."

A fiery flush swept Reece's face. "When have you known Utah to be meek?"

Tennie laughed. "Let me guess. He said something along these lines." Her voice dropped to an amazing likeness of Utah's deep drawl. "If my Celeste wants a grandchild, by hell, son, you should give her one. Go out and find yourself some sweet young thing and wed her and bed her, and not particularly in that order." Tennie imitated Utah's booming laughter. "I missed having a child of my own, but the thought of grandchildren running all over the house can bring a tear to this old man's eye, son."

Reece applauded. "Remarkable, Tennie. Are you sure you weren't there when that speech was given? You had it nearly perfect."

"Only *nearly* perfect?" She frowned. Uncle Utah had been one of her favorites to imitate since she was ten. "What did I miss?"

"You missed the part where he offered to adopt me so the grandchild would bear the Montgomery name."

Tennie slowly shook her head and chuckled. "I should have seen that one coming." She gazed at Reece. "I hope you told him to stuff it."

"Those weren't my exact words." Reece grinned. "But he got my message loud and clear."

"Good. If you don't stand up to Uncle Utah, he'll walk all over you."

"I noticed that trait in him—and the rest of the Montgomery clan."

Her delicately arched brow shot back up. "Really?"

Reece's grin couldn't have gotten any larger. "Really."

Tennie huffed, but lowered her brow. The man was absolutely correct. Montgomerys tended to be a pushy lot. Piqued at his observation she sweetly asked, "So what did you find out about the murder?"

Reece conceded defeat for the moment and allowed the grin to disappear. "Not much more than what Aunt Maine told me on the phone. A guy named Tailpipe met the underside of a pickup truck and lost. The locals are blaming your uncle Colorado because presumably he was fooling around with Tailpipe's wife, Emma Sue."

"You don't think it was a faulty hydraulic lift?"

"Nope." Reece stepped over the pile of junk on the floor and paced back to the window. "Your family wouldn't have pulled this reunion with such a shoddy ending. The lift had to be tampered with." His fingers played with the drapes as he stared off into the night. "The first place we need to go is the garage."

"Being the scene of the murder, it's roped off to the general public."

Reece glanced over his shoulder and frowned. "Damn."

Tennie smiled sweetly. "We have permission to examine the site at ten o'clock tomorrow morning. I had to promise that we wouldn't fiddle with the lift, though. A specialist from the manufacturer will be here tomorrow afternoon and will be issuing a report on his findings."

"Another actor?"

"Of course. If there wasn't a real murder, how could the lift fail?"

"I really wish that one year your family would hold its reunion at the scene of a real murder so we wouldn't have to figure out who were actors and who were real players."

"Don't you think that would be depressing?" Tennie sadly shook her head. "How can we have a great time if someone really dies?"

Reece thought about having the entire Montgomery family at the scene of a real murder and shuddered. The Montgomerys invented the word competitiveness. Now the reunions were sort of laid back with everyone having a good time, visiting, sightseeing, and polishing up on their detective skills. The only one besides himself who relished the win was Tennie. She was born and bred a Montgomery. It seemed to irk her no end to see a Carpenter solve the mystery. "You have a point there." A frown pulled at his mouth. "How did we end up with permission to visit the scene?"

"Jake the Fake."

"Ah, yes. Good old Jake the Fake." The frown deepened. "Care to elaborate on how you know he's a fake, and why he's granting us permission to visit the scene of the crime?"

"It didn't take a genius to figure out he's a fake. The man doesn't know his penal code. Actors playing the more complicated roles are easier to detect. It's the ones playing ordinary people feeding you a bunch of false clues that are harder to recognize."

"So how come he invited us to visit the garage?"

"I hinted that I'd be in town around ten tomorrow morning."

"And?"

"That I would love to see the inside of the garage."

"And?"

Her smile slipped a notch. "Did I mention his overactive hormones?"

Reece thrust a hand through his hair. "Does Jake the Fake know I'll be with you?"

"I seemed to have forgotten that piece of information."

"Great. You seduced a cop."

"He's not a cop and I didn't seduce him."

"What would you call it?"

"Asking nicely. He's an actor paid to play a certain part. As far as I know he's being paid to distract me."

Reece glanced at her in disbelief. She was curled up in the chair like a little girl all warm and cuddly in her oversize sweat suit. Her face was bare of any makeup and not one flash of jewelry distracted from her beauty. Her long golden hair was haphazardly pulled back and tied with a white silky ribbon. Hazel eyes gleamed with intelligence, mystery, and a touch of vulnerability. Tennessee was the most vibrant woman he had ever encountered. The thought of paying someone to woo her was preposterous. She didn't realize her own appeal and that was what made her so dangerous. Any man who backed off because of the career she had chosen was a fool. Reece pulled his mind off such an alarming path. "What do you think he'll do when I show up with you?"

"What can he do? Nothing. He'll act the part he's being paid to play."

"What about your uncle Colorado?"

"He's being held at the local jail. Bail hasn't been set yet."

"Can we visit him?"

"Only between the hours of ten and six." Tennie stood up and dumped the contents of her small clutch purse on the table beside the chair. She plucked out a crinkled napkin. "Here it is."

Reece bent and retrieved a roll of hard candy that had fallen off the table. "What's that?" He leaned over her shoulder.

"The layout of Little Lincoln." She carefully unfolded the napkin to reveal an ink-drawn map. "If you drove in from the airport, you had to go down Main Street to get here." Her finger followed a long ink slash. "Here's the garage," her finger moved about two inches farther, "and here's the sheriff's office."

"What's the *X* on Mary Todd Avenue?"

"That's Emma Sue's house."

Reece moved his finger to another *X*. "And this one on Presidential Boulevard?"

"That's the home of Tailpipe's mistress."

"He had a mistress?" Reece asked in surprise.

"So I gathered. Problem is she's married."

"To whom?" The enticing fragrance of Tennie's shampoo stirred his senses. Her body was mere inches away. One more step and she would be in his arms.

"The man who is the local beer distributor." She pointed to another *X*. "Here. His name is Ralph Stone and his wife is Pricilla."

His voice deepened as his body tensed with desire. "Are they all actors?"

"Don't know yet. We'll find out tomorrow."

"What's this last *X* for?" He purposely brushed her arm and entered the danger zone by stepping closer. His senses went into overdrive. Her sweat suit smelled of fabric softener, her lips hinted at the mint toothpaste she must have used moments ago, and a lingering trace of sandalwood perfume still remained behind her ear. The warmth of her body seemed to scorch his chest.

Tennie glanced up at Reece. "That's where I can buy a set of long johns and some decent underwear."

"You asked Jake where you could buy underwear?" Reece's voice boomed against the walls. Anyone staying within four rooms of Tennie's would have surely heard his shouting.

Her shoulder and arm brushed his chest as she tried to turn around. Reece had her pinned between the small table and his chest. She fought the wave of desire surging through her veins at his nearness. "Don't be an idiot, Reece. Do I seem reckless enough to ask a strange man where to buy underwear?"

He shifted his weight in closer. His body was naturally responding to the feminine fire he detected burning brightly beneath her professional image. His gaze locked onto the tempting moistness of her lower lip. "Did you say reckless?"

Tennie noticed the hungry darkening of his eyes and swallowed hard. Reece Carpenter had stepped out of his role. He was no longer a cousin-by-marriage. He was a man, basic and simple. Her gaze lowered to his mouth. The sensual fullness of his lower lip begged to be explored. Her small pink tongue lightly licked a path over her upper lip in anticipation. "Reckless?"

Reece's ravenous gaze followed the delicate tongue on its sensual journey. His emotions overruled his common sense as he slowly lowered his head. The need to taste those sweet dewy lips became essential. He smiled slightly. "Definitely reckless."

Her tender sigh of wonder feathered across his mouth as the telephone began to ring.

Tennie jumped back nearly knocking over the table.

Reece muttered a curse and stepped away, dragging a trembling hand through his hair.

Tennie picked up the phone on the third ring. "Hello?" Her voice was uneven and raspy.

She watched Reece walk over to the connecting door as the caller talked.

"No, Montana, you didn't wake me."

She bit her lower lip as Reece walked through and softly closed the door behind him.

"No, no. Nothing like that, big brother." Sadly she added, "I was just being a little reckless, that's all."

THREE

Tennie glanced over at Reece, who was sitting behind the steering wheel scowling. They were slowly and cautiously making their way down the steep road from the lodge to the town of Little Lincoln. Tennie wanted to scream in frustration or at least jam the four-wheel-drive Jeep into third gear and tear down the mountain road like a bat out of hell. Her energy level was revving, ready to explode, and her output was a mere trickle. Reece was driving the Jeep as if he were in the race with the tortoise and the hare, and he was the tortoise. "Can't this thing go any faster?"

Reece kept his eyes straight ahead. "The road's still covered with morning dew. It might be slippery."

Two sentences! Reece had finally spoken two whole sentences to her this morning. When she'd walked into the dining room earlier, he had politely excused himself and moved to her uncle Utah and aunt Florida's table. She had relieved her brother, Montana, of his three rambunctious boys and headed for the buffet table. Montana very thankfully had loaded up a tray to take back to Sue Ellen and their sleeping newborn son. Six-year-old Austin, four-year-old Dallas, and two-year-old Houston thoroughly enjoyed the breakfast Tennie had concocted for them. Sunny-side-up eggs for eyes, bacon mouths, half banana noses, and blueberry muffin ears overflowed their plates and stomachs.

When it was time to leave for town she turned the boys over to her mother and headed for the parking lot. If Reece wanted to ignore her, that was fine with her. She had a murder to solve. She just had put the key into the ignition of her rental Jeep when Reece appeared by her side and insisted on driving.

She glanced out the window and frowned at the scenery going by. A slug could make it into town faster. "There is a gas pedal, you know."

Reece's hands tightened on the wheel. "Not everyone is as reckless as you are."

Tennie's gaze flew to his mouth. Even frowning it was the most sensual mouth she had ever encountered. She had wanted that kiss last night as much as she had wanted the one in the basement ten months ago. She didn't understand this attraction for Reece, but she knew a kiss could cure it. He would kiss her and she would realize he kissed like any other man and the attraction would fade. Plain and simple. It was the not knowing that heightened the emotions. Tennie hated a mystery. One kiss and poof, he would become Reece the rival again. She turned away to stare back out the side window, muttering, "Yeah, tell me about it."

Reece slammed on the brakes and the Jeep jerked to a sudden stop in the middle of the road. In a flash he had his seat belt and hers undone and was hauling her over the gear shift and into his lap. His hungry mouth claimed hers before she could utter a sound.

Tennie melted into his arms like pistachio ice cream in July. The kiss immediately softened: The sensual birth of ecstasy. She answered his deep groan with a gentle sigh as her arms tightened around his neck. Her tongue boldly thrust forward and entwined with his. Warmth invaded her and her blood started to sing as it rushed through her body. Time shattered into fragments of nothingness as the kiss lengthened.

Tennie felt herself being swept up into a haze of need and passion. Desire rode the wave of delight as she answered every one of the demands Reece's mouth made.

Reece felt the throbbing hardness of his desire and the sweet seductive surrender of Tennie in his arms. What in the hell was he doing kissing Tennie? He tore his mouth away from her intoxicating sweetness and picked her up and plopped her back down into her own seat.

Tennie's hands fell uselessly onto her lap as she blinked in astonishment.

Reece tore his gaze away from Tennie's startled and

vulnerable expression and jammed his hands through his hair. Lord, how he wanted her. He still could feel the heat where her fingers had caressed his neck and the fire that raced through his veins. His voice was rough and uneven as he snapped out, "*That* should not have happened."

Her eyes narrowed fractionally and her fingers tightened into two small fists. *Wasn't he the one who hauled me into his arms and proceeded to kiss me into next week? And now he has the gall to say it shouldn't have happened!* "You're damn right it shouldn't have." *Grandmom Pinky would never forgive me if I blackened one of his eyes.*

Reece stared incredulously back at her. "*Now* you agree with me?" There was a slight edge of hurt to his question.

"Wasn't I supposed to?" Unexpected tears started to blur her vision.

"Of course you were. It just surprised me, that's all. In the two years that I've known you, you haven't agreed with me once on any issue."

Tennie fixed her collar on her coat and zipped the zipper all the way up. "In those two years I've only been in your company for about fifteen days." She straightened the huge canvas carryall she called a purse that was lying at her feet. "I'm sure eventually we would have agreed on something." She dug through the bag and yanked out a pair of sunglasses and put them on. She refastened the seat belt and stared straight ahead. They definitely shouldn't have kissed. Of course their reasons for agreeing on that conclusion were entirely different. Reece was probably harboring feelings along the lines of her being his cousin-by-marriage and Utah's goddaughter, while hers centered around the kiss itself. That certainly wasn't some ordinary kiss they had just shared. Frogs had been known to turn into princes with such kisses. Reece wasn't a prince in disguise and this definitely wasn't some fairy tale with happily-ever-after printed on the last page. This was reality, and reality didn't give Tennie princes, just the frogs.

He noticed the protective barriers she was building around herself and frowned. Since when did Tennie need barriers? "If you showed up at more of your family's get-togethers, instead of hiding in some hick town, we probably could have been friends by now and your grandfather wouldn't have to blackmail us into working together." He had plagued every family get-together for the last ten months hoping to see her.

"Hick town?" She tightened her grip around the heavy straps of her bag. *Make that two black eyes and a fat lip.*

"Okay, maybe that was uncalled for, but I've never had the privilege of visiting Hogs Hollow, Iowa, yet. But from what your family tells me it's not a booming metropolis."

"If I wanted a booming metropolis, I would have moved to New York or L.A. I happen to love Hogs Hollow."

"Why didn't you stay in Sacramento or at least

California?" He had always wondered why Tennie had left the golden state and her family to settle somewhere in the bread basket of America.

"Because I didn't want to," Tennie snapped. It was none of his business why she moved. She looked straight ahead.

"Uncle Utah was right. You're independent, head strong—"

"Which one of those qualities don't you like?"

"I didn't say I don't appreciate certain qualities in a person."

"So"—she arched one delicate brow and smiled sweetly—"which one scares you? The independent streak that runs very wide and long through all Montgomerys or the keen intelligence or quick wit?" Eyes narrowed, she studied his expression. "It can't be the name Montgomery. An ace detective like yourself wouldn't be afraid of a simple name—covet it, perhaps, but be scared of it? Never."

Reece flushed with the memory of how he was so in awe of his new stepfather, Utah, when he first met him.

Tennie noticed the flush. "It won't work, Reece."

"What won't work?"

"You, me." She spread her hands. "Us."

Confused, he asked, "What are you talking about?"

She started to dig through her purse looking for a pair of gloves. The calendar might say it was spring, but someone had obviously forgotten to tell the weather. She pulled out one expensive red leather glove and one fuzzy purple mitten with a snowman knitted into it. She put on the two mismatched gloves. "Look, Reece, you're already into the family, so there's no need to push it any further."

Reece drummed his fingers on the steering wheel and stared at the stubborn tilt of her jaw. "Tell me you're joking."

"I'm joking," she said sweetly. "Now can we get going? I would like to solve this murder before losing a limb to frostbite."

He fastened his seat belt and shifted the Jeep into first gear without taking his gaze from her face. She was serious. She honestly thought he had kissed her because she was a Montgomery. He turned his attention back to the road and proceeded down the mountain with a tad more speed than before. If he was smart, he would allow her to go on believing that was the reason he had kissed her. It was a hell of a lot safer than admitting how much he really wanted her.

By the time he drove into the town of Little Lincoln he was positive that was the way he was going to go. The kiss would be forgotten, Tennie would think he was a jerk, and life within the Montgomery clan would return to normal.

"It's right up the street." Tennie pointed straight ahead at a faded, bent, and rusty sign that at one time must have read *Taylor's Garage*. Now it read *a lor's Gar*. "See it?"

Reece slowed down. "Yes." He pulled into the decrepit parking lot and groaned when the front wheel jammed into a monster-size pothole. "Tailpipe obviously didn't believe in sinking any money into his business."

Tennie glanced at the run-down building in front of them and laughed. "Where did they find such a place?" Two rusty old cars that looked as though they'd been firebombed acted as matching bookends for the empty oil cans and spare car parts littering the parking lot. A huge dirty plate glass window of the office was cracked and boasted more silver tape than an entire air-conditioning system. All in all, Tailpipe had a charming little two-bay garage. Tennie opened her door and stepped out as Jake pulled into the parking lot right behind them.

Reece frowned in disgust at the filthy building in front of him and scowled at the young cop smiling at Tennie as if he hadn't eaten in a week and she was a choice cut of prime rib. He got out of the Jeep and slowly made his way over to Tennie and the hungry cop.

"Reece," said Tennie, "have you met Officer Altman yet?"

"We saw each other yesterday at the lodge, but I don't think we were properly introduced." Jake held out his hand and flashed a toothy grin at Reece.

Reece shook his hand and returned the grin with an equally false one. "Reece Carpenter."

"Carpenter?" Jake looked at Tennie. "He's not a Montgomery?"

"He's my cousin," Tennie said.

"By marriage," added Reece, with a hint of impatience. "My mother married her uncle Utah three years ago."

Jake gazed between Tennie and Reece and slowly smiled. "I see." He walked over to the door and unlocked it. "You came along with Tennie to see how a great detective works."

Tennie tried to smother a chuckle with the purple mitten.

Reece's back stiffened and a red haze blurred his vision. Jake the Fake had just landed a perfect bull's-eye. "No. I came along with Tennie because we are partners."

"Partners!" Jake glanced at Tennie. "Really? I never heard of a Montgomery working with a partner before." He stepped into the garage and flipped on the overhead lights.

Horrified, Tennie said, "I certainly didn't ask for him."

It was Reece's turn to chuckle at the priceless look on Tennie's face. Jake the Fake had better run because Tennie appeared to be ready to deck him. Reece followed Jake into the garage and gazed around. The place was a mess. If there was a system to Tailpipe's madness, it wasn't evident to Reece. He cautiously walked around the small filthy office, trying to hold his breath. The overpowering stench of oil, grease, and turpentine was enough to knock him over.

Tennie continued to glare at Jake and Reece as she stepped into the office and frowned at the girly pinup calendar on the far wall. Tailpipe obviously had a fascination with Miss January because here it was April and she was still decorating the office. Tennie looked around, nudging one or two coffee cups with the toe of her sneaker.

Jake found a relatively clean spot on the doorframe and leaned against it. He watched Reece and Tennie as they explored the room from top to bottom. "You won't find anything interesting."

Tennie quickly skimmed through a pile of bills sitting on the desk. They were mostly second and third notices with a couple of threats from collection agencies thrown in for good measure. "What makes you say that, Jake?"

"We went through this place with a fine-tooth comb. Nothing's here except bills, trash, and more bills." He watched as Tennie bent over and picked up a piece of paper that had slid under a pair of used snow tires stacked under the window. "What's that?"

Tennie glanced at the paper and then quickly back at Jake. "Nothing. It's only another letter from the electric company telling him they will cut off his service if they don't receive their money immediately."

Jake chuckled and lit a cigarette. "Tailpipe wasn't known to pay his bills on time."

Tennie met Reece's gaze and carefully placed the letter on the desk so he could see it. It was a copy of an invoice for work performed on Colorado's car. She casually walked to the other side of the room and started to read the assortment of business cards tacked to the wall.

Reece quickly read the invoice then looked at Jake who was studying Tennie. "Am I allowed to look in the desk?"

"Sure, nothing in there but paper clips and more bills."

Reece opened the top drawer. Filthy rubber bands, bent paper clips, some pennies, and a half-empty roll of antacid tablets filled the small tray in the front of the drawer. Grease-smudged papers were jammed into the back part. Reece quickly went through the papers. More bills and notices. He shut the drawer and opened the top one of the three bordering the kneehole. A ripped greasy telephone book and a few matchbooks, advertising how to become a truck driver at home, were all that he found.

He opened the next drawer. Two screwdrivers and a pair of vise grips rattled around. The third drawer was locked. "What's in here, Jake?"

Tennie and Jake turned around and looked at Reece. Jake chuckled. "The key's under the paper clips in the top drawer."

Reece found the key and unlocked the drawer. Tennie walked over and glanced down into the drawer. She sighed in disgust and Jake kept on chuckling. Reece hauled out three years' worth of girly magazines. They were well thumbed and dog-eared. He dumped them back into the drawer and slammed it shut.

Jake glanced at Reece and winked. "He read them for the articles."

Tennie walked out of the office and into the garage area. The two bays stood empty and the lift was in the lowered position. Someone had taken a can of white spray paint and outlined the figure of a body on the greasy garage floor. Her family's sense of humor could really be morbid at times. She glanced over her shoulder at Jake. "Who found the body?"

"A waitress from Sadie's Diner."

"What's her name?" Reece asked.

"Pricilla Stone. She works the morning shift. Five till eleven, six days a week."

Reece and Tennie exchanged glances. Pricilla was supposed to be Tailpipe's mistress. "Was it her truck that fell on him?" asked Tennie.

"Nope, she drives a big fat Cadillac that's older than most of the residents of Little Lincoln. Tailpipe worked on that car two or three times a week just to keep it going." Jake dropped his cigarette butt onto the floor and stepped on it. "Barely a day went by that you wouldn't have seen Pricilla's big old fat Caddy parked in here."

Reece studied the outline painted on the floor. "Whose truck was it that did old Tailpipe in?"

"That's the funny part." Tennie and Reece both stopped their snooping and looked at Jake. "It was Pricilla's husband, Ralph's truck." Tennie raised an eyebrow at Jake and he continued, "Ralph never brought his truck to Tailpipe to fix. He always drove it into Pine Bluff to that fancy dealership that opened about ten years ago. Only the best would do for Ralph's truck."

"Didn't it strike you as odd that the first time Tail-pipe worked on Ralph's truck it killed him?" Reece asked.

"Lord," chuckled Jake, "you think Ralph did it." He slowly shook his head. "If you would have seen Ralph when he found out his pickup plummeted six feet to the ground when the lift failed, you would know it couldn't have been him. Ralph would rather shoot his own foot off than dent one corner panel of his precious truck."

"You dropped Ralph from your list of suspects because of his affections for his pickup truck?" asked Tennie.

"Sorry to disappoint you Ms. Montgomery, but there wasn't any list. Your uncle Colorado is our one and only suspect. He's our man all right."

"Do you have an eye witness?"

"No, but we do have a reliable witness who's pretty sure he saw your uncle around here the morning of the murder."

"You're holding my uncle on a *'pretty sure'* he might have been in this area sometime that morn-ing?"

"Yes, and I must say your uncle has been a model prisoner."

Tennie stepped over part of an engine and eyed the fan belts and hoses hanging on the back wall.

"When did you say my uncle would appear in front of the judge for bail?"

"Wednesday morning. Judge Riddle is on a fishing trip and won't be back until then."

"Can I visit Colorado this afternoon?"

"When you finish up in here, I could take you right over to see him."

Jake's smile prompted Reece to take a couple of protective steps closer to Tennie. "That's awful nice of you, Jake, but I need to talk to Colorado too."

Tennie bit the inside of her cheek to keep from screaming at their macho game. Jake had as much class as a dime store ring at a charity ball and Reece wasn't cut out to be a Sir Galahad, or maybe she wasn't cut out to play the damsel in distress. Whatever the reason, both men were starting to get on her nerves. "Thanks for the offer, Jake, but I need to stop at the diner first. I'm starved."

Reece glanced questioningly at Tennie. Hadn't she just packed away a breakfast that looked like a poster of don'ts from the American Heart Association. Crisp bacon, a mound of scrambled eggs, and brown sugary muffins loaded with butter. Where were the fruits, the fresh-squeezed juices, and the oat bran muffins? Tennie was a walking gastronomic nightmare and she wanted to repeat the performance.

Tennie smiled sweetly at Jake and kicked Reece in the shins.

Reece glared at Tennie as he rubbed the aching spot.

"Didn't you promise me something to eat on the way into town?" Tennie asked Reece.

He tried to decipher the message burning in Tennie's gaze. "Sure did, Tennie." He rubbed his shin again. "I just didn't realize how hungry you were."

She laughed softly and turned to face Jake. "I get a trifle cranky if I don't have my morning allotment of coffee."

Jake's face looked ready to explode from holding in the laughter. "I'm sure Juan Valdez appreciates the job security."

Reece muttered something about her being cranky under his breath. He glanced around the garage one last time. "Are you ready to leave, Tennie? We aren't going to find anything here. The police already have been through this place and haven't come up with a thing."

Jake's chest expanded another inch. "That's right, Ms. Montgomery. There isn't a clue to be had within a hundred yards of this place."

She looked at the hydraulic lift. "You did say the expert will be coming in this afternoon to take a look at the lift, didn't you?"

"Yes. Later tonight I'll deliver a copy of his report out to the lodge if you'd like."

"That would be wonderful." Tennie beamed. "Did I properly thank you yet for the copy of the autopsy and the police report I received this morning?"

A dark flush stained Jake's cheeks. "It was my pleasure."

Reece groaned with disgust. By the smitten look Jake was wearing he was liable to deliver every folder in the police station to her. "Are you ready to leave, Tennie?"

She glanced at her hands and wiggled her nose. "Let me wash my hands first." She walked around the white outline of a body on the cement floor and headed toward a small cubbyhole of a room squeezed between the office and metal racks holding spare car parts.

Tennie found the light switch and glanced around the room with distaste. And to think people actually had the gall to comment on her housekeeping. The mere thought of washing her hands in the grime-encrusted sink brought a wave of nausea. She reached for a paper towel and wiped her hands while glancing around. Every square inch of the walls was covered with centerfolds. Using the paper towel she opened the medicine cabinet above the sink. An empty box of bandages and a bottle of iodine sat on the top shelf. The second shelf held a nearly empty bottle of inexpensive after-shave, a used razor, and a shaving brush. The bottom shelf was empty except for a pack of matches. Tennie picked up the matches and examined the cover. The After Six Motel promised confidentiality, clean sheets, and hourly rates.

Tennie slid the matches into the back pocket of her jeans and shook her head in amazement. Tailpipe Taylor's autopsy report clearly stated he was seventy-two years old. Either her family was slipping up when it came to clues, or Tailpipe was one amazing character. She turned off the light and joined Reece who was standing by the office door.

Reece noticed the laughter in Tennie's eyes and frowned. Why did he always feel he was missing something important when she was around? "Ready?"

"Yeah, but I want to look around outside first, okay?"

Reece opened the door. "Sure." He glanced over at Jake who was leaning against the desk. "Thanks for letting us come in, Jake."

"Yes, Jake. Thank you very much." Tennie couldn't prevent a small chuckle from escaping. "It was very interesting."

Jake tipped his hat. "It was my pleasure, Ms. Montgomery."

"Call me Tennie, Jake. I have a feeling we will be seeing more of each other."

Jake raised an eyebrow and Reece scowled as he hauled Tennie out the door. As the door closed behind them, Reece demanded, "What in the hell does that mean?"

"What?" She started to walk through the parking lot, examining the trash.

"That part about seeing Jake more."

"Oh, that." Tennie made her way around the side of the building, kicking cans and shuffling loose papers with the toe of her sneaker. "He's obviously one of the key players in this murder. I'm sure he'll be around till the end."

Reece stomped after her. "Why in the hell did you kick me?"

"Because I wanted you not Jake, to take me to the diner." She bent down and studied the dirt near the back door of the garage. The only footprints she could detect appeared to have been made by a raccoon. "Whoever fiddled with the lift came and went by the front door."

He half smiled. "You prefer my company over Jake's?" He couldn't have cared less if an entire marching band paraded through the garage on the day Tailpipe bought the farm.

"It's not a question of whose company I prefer." She rose up and started to head back to the parking lot. "I didn't want Jake around when we met Pricilla Stone. People tend to be close mouthed around cops." She glanced at her watch. "She will be about to finish her shift when we get there. Maybe we can persuade her to have a cup of coffee with us."

Reece's smile died as he watched Tennie climb into the Jeep.

Jake watched as the Jeep backed out of the parking lot and headed into town. He chuckled at some private joke and reached for the thick black rotary phone sitting on the desk. He dialed a number form memory.

"Hello, it's me." He waited a second, grinning. "Yeah, yeah, they just left." He reached into his shirt pocket and pulled out a pack of cigarettes. "All's going as planned." He lit a cigarette and blew out the match. "They're headed for Sadie's now. Tennie was quick enough to pick up on the fact that Pricilla was there." He blew a smoke ring and watched as it rose toward the ceiling. "I'm afraid Reece has it bad. He wouldn't have noticed Tailpipe's body lying on the floor, let alone any evidence. The only thing Reece was studying was Tennie." Another smoke ring floated heavenward. "No, no, trust me, they didn't suspect a thing."

Jake watched as a car pulled into the parking lot and three females emerged. Colors in every conceivable combination brightened the parking lot as they made their way toward the door. "I've got to go. Florida and her daughters pulled in." He laughed and stomped out the cigarette. "Yes, sir, I have my sunglasses ready." Jake hung up the phone and studied the identical twins who looked amazingly like Michelle Pfeiffer after some crazed wardrobe person got a hold of her. He pushed himself away from the desk and muttered, "Decisions, decisions, how am I ever going to choose?"

Florida Montgomery-Smyth threw open the door to the office and burst in. A teal-colored parka and a canary-yellow boa accented her red latex stretch pants and black ankle boots. For a woman in her late forties, she carried the combination off extremely well. "There you are Officer Altman. We've been looking for you all morning."

❖————————❖

"Not here," Tennie yelled.

Reece jammed on the brakes and came to a sudden stop in the middle of the diner parking lot. "Why not? It's close to the door."

"Pull around back."

He drove the Jeep past six empty parking spaces before Tennie pointed and said, "There."

He pulled into the space. "Why this one?"

Tennie opened her door and was out in a flash. "You stand guard. Tell me when someone comes."

"What are you doing?" he asked in alarm as she opened the door of the car next to them. It had to be Pricilla's big old Caddy. He hurried around the Jeep and started to pull Tennie out of the front seat. "Get out of there. That's breaking and entering."

Tennie pushed aside bubble gum wrappers, empty breath mint boxes, two issues of *Cosmopolitan*, sparkling red sunglasses, and six country and western cassettes. "Shhh . . . Just keep an eye out."

Reece clamped his hand onto her thigh and tugged. "Tennie, come on now. . . ."

She reached over and opened the glove compartment. More papers, maps, trash, and cassettes. She slammed the door shut and was reaching under the seat when Reece yanked her from the car, softly closed the door, and pressed her against the side of the Caddy. Before she could protest his mouth covered hers.

Tennie felt herself melting into the steel frame of the car. Distant voices registered in her brain, but she didn't pay any attention to what they were saying.

She was too engrossed in the way Reece was kissing her. She had only been kissed like this once before in her life, this morning in the front seat of the Jeep. Enchanted kisses weren't an everyday occurrence for her, and she wanted to relish this one.

Reece heard the voices fade and a car start up and drive away. He slowly broke the kiss and stared down into Tennie's exquisite face. She was breathtaking.

Tennie reached up and lightly traced Reece's lower lip with the tip of her trembling finger. "Reece?"

He read the desire in her gaze and swallowed hard. "Hmmm. . . ."

"You don't kiss like a frog at all."

FOUR

Tennie alternated her attention between the plastic-coated menu in her hands and the intriguing atmosphere of Sadie's Diner. Anything was better than looking at the man sitting across from her grinning like a Cheshire cat. Someone would think the man had won the million-dollar lottery instead of merely kissing her as a distraction in the parking lot. How was she supposed to have known someone had been coming?

She had picked out Pricilla Stone the moment they entered the diner. Tennie had purposely steered Reece in the direction of the booths the woman seemed to be working. Within moments she had strolled over to their booth, presented them with menus, and announced her name was Pricilla, and she was their waitress. Tennie silently patted herself on her back for picking Pricilla out from the other four waitresses. Tailpipe's mistress was a sight to behold. She was dressed in the same faded pink uniform as the other waitresses, but that was where the similarities ended. Pricilla had the top two buttons of the uniform undone and had a leopard print silk scarf wrapped around her neck with its ends snuggled deep between her ample breasts. She wore more makeup than Tammy Faye Bakker and a pair of sparkling pink horn-rimmed glasses was perched on her nose. Her silver hair, piled on top of her head in a ridiculous fluff, reflected the pink of her uniform. Her entire head reminded Tennie of swirls of pink cotton candy. Pricilla sounded like a one-man band when she walked. Bracelets clanged, necklaces jingled, and huge boulder-size dangling earrings knocked against her shoulders. Her eye-popping pink lipstick matched the blush stroked across her pale cheeks and the overpowering smell of inexpensive perfume moved in a cloud around her. Pricilla Stone was definitely a colorful character and the perfect woman to play Tailpipe's mistress. Tennie watched as she walked away to take another order.

Loud conversations overrode the jangling of silverware and the gentle clanking of thick stoneware plates. The aroma of recently brewed coffee and the enticing smell of freshly baked bread caused Tennie's stomach to rumble with anticipation. She studied the menu and dwindled down her choices to six possibilities.

"So, if I don't kiss like a frog, what do I kiss like?" asked Reece. He was pretty sure logic would say a prince, but with Tennie one could never be sure.

Tennie glanced up from the menu and narrowed

her eyes. His silly grin hadn't faded one iota. "You must have misunderstood me." She still couldn't believe she had actually said that to him.

Reece arched one brow and continued grinning. "What did you say then?"

"I don't remember"—she glanced back down at the menu—"something about the fog."

He bit the inside of his cheek to keep from laughing. Tennie was adorable when her back was pinned against the wall and she was trying to bluff her way out. "Tennie, there wasn't any fog."

"What do you think I was trying to tell you?" She turned her head and smiled pleasantly at Pricilla as she approached their booth.

With pencil poised, Pricilla asked, "What will it be?"

Tennie gave an order that would have made a lumberjack proud. Pricilla's fingers flew over the order pad. When she finally stopped she gazed quizzically at Tennie for a moment before turning to the other occupant in the booth. "And you, handsome?"

Reece had been too occupied studying Tennie to read a menu. His fascination with the flush staining her delicate cheeks caused him to miss whatever it was she had ordered. Not wanting to look like an idiot, he said, "I'll have the same thing."

Pricilla's pencil hesitated a brief moment before scribbling something on the pad. She glanced once more at the unusual couple. "I'll be right back with your coffee."

Reece's gaze followed her as she went behind the counter and picked up the coffeepot. He frowned as she whispered something to one of the other waitresses, who turned and stared at him and Tennie. He didn't like the feeling clutching at his gut. "Tennie?"

She marked her place with a finger and glanced up from the maze printed on her paper place mat. She had been three quarters of the way through. "Yeah?"

"What did you order?"

"Lunch." She went back to doing the maze. The cute little puppy was only a few twists and turns from finding his bone.

Reece glanced at the clock on the far wall. It was a few minutes before eleven, surely it wasn't that unusual to have someone order an early lunch. He kept his gaze on the flamboyant Pricilla. "So that's Tailpipe's mistress."

"*Was*, as in the past tense. Remember?" Tennie's finger reached the bone without detours.

"Do you think she's an actress?"

She glanced over at the woman in question and grinned. "What do you think?"

"Definitely."

She chuckled. "Smart boy." Her gaze went to the secret message printed next to the maze and she started to decode it.

"Do you want me to invite her to join us for a cup of coffee after her shift is over?"

Tennie's gaze leapt between Pricilla and Reece.

"Sure, go ahead." So far she'd decoded the words, *Be smart and drink.* . . . "But don't be surprised if she gets the idea you're trying to pick her up."

Reece looked horrified by the idea. "Why would she think that?"

"It's the role she's playing." *Your milk.* Tennie grimaced at the secret message. What else could she expect from a family restaurant; *Be smart and drink your Wild Turkey*? "Pricilla's playing the role of the mistress. She would naturally assume every male making polite conversation with her would want what Tailpipe was getting."

Reece glanced at Pricilla and the extravagant way she swung her hips as she made her way back over to their table, topping off other customers' cups with fresh coffee and provocative remarks. He swallowed hard. "Tennie?"

"Hmmm . . ." She had disregarded the place mat and was studying the people around them.

"Would you ask Pricilla to join us?"

She grinned. "Sure."

Pricilla stepped over to their table and placed two coffee cups down. "Is regular okay, or should I shake my bootie back over there and pick up the decaf?"

Tennie grinned. "If it doesn't have caffeine, I don't want it."

Pricilla's laugh sounded like a pack of baboons on a feeding frenzy. "What about you, handsome, are you up for some stimulation?"

Reece cast Tennie a desperate look before answering. "Regular coffee will be fine." He lightly kicked Tennie underneath the table and jerked his head in Pricilla's direction.

Tennie kicked him back and smiled with satisfaction when he jumped in his seat. "Pricilla, I was wondering if you would consider joining us for a cup of coffee when you're through with your shift."

Pricilla's gaze brightened. "You mean like one of those French things, a ménage à trois?"

Tennie's smile widened as Reece spilled the entire packet of sugar he was about to pour into his coffee. "No, Pricilla. We are relatives of Colorado Montgomery and we are trying to solve the murder of Tailpipe Taylor." Her voice lowered with due sympathy. "We understand you knew Mr. Taylor quite well."

Pricilla puffed out her ample chest and lightly patted the swirl of cotton candy on top of her head. "What I don't know about Tailpipe"—she quickly crossed herself—"God rest his soul, ain't worth knowing." She gave Reece a wink. "Right, sweetie?"

Reece mumbled something and kept his gaze on his coffee cup.

"Well, I don't rightly know if I should talk to you at all, being kin to Colorado and all." She swept up the sugar Reece had spilled. "That man murdered the most fun I had in this here town since the circus passed this way back in '64."

"Colorado didn't kill anyone," Tennie said.

"The police say he did."

"We're going to prove he didn't, Pricilla. Wouldn't you like to help us find the real killer?"

Pricilla glanced at the clock. "I'll be finished up in about twenty minutes. I'll join you then." She waltzed away filling customers' cups with the remaining coffee.

Reece looked at Tennie. "You really aren't going to believe anything that woman says, are you?"

Tennie took a sip of her coffee and considered his question. "About as much as I'll believe what anyone else in this town tells us. Pricilla's playing her part, and I must say she's doing it admirably."

"How can you say that?"

"She has you so nervous that you won't even look at her, let alone ask her any questions. If she pulls this same number on the other male members of the family, over half of the Montgomerys will miss getting some very valuable clues."

Disturbed that she was partially right, he asked, "How do you know they are going to be valuable clues?"

"Because she wouldn't be going through all this trouble to discourage you if they weren't." Tennie gave him a sad little smile as if to say it was the most basic observation.

Reece was still trying to figure out where he went wrong when Pricilla returned to their table carrying a huge round tray loaded with food. In disbelief he sat there and watched as she unloaded platters of cheeseburgers, fries, and chicken wings smothered in hot sauce. Bowls of coleslaw and applesauce were squeezed onto the table along with two of the biggest pieces of chocolate cake he had ever seen.

Pricilla briskly rubbed her hands together and admired the jammed table. "I had a bet going with one of the other waitresses that I could make it all fit." She glanced at Reece, "I just won myself a free bikini wax at Jolene's Beauty Shop." She winked suggestively. "It would be a shame to allow such a prize to go unnoticed." Pricilla's gaze skimmed the width of Reece's shoulders. "Now, sugar, you go ahead and dig right on in." She tugged at her uniform that had bunched around her hips. "I'll be back in two shakes of a lambie-pie's tail." With a swish of pink uniform she returned to her other customers.

Tennie chuckled as she bit into a cheeseburger with the works. Reece's face was redder than some fire trucks she had seen. She took another bite and noticed he wasn't eating. "Something the matter with your food?"

Reece gazed in front of him and didn't have any idea where to start. Breakfast was only three hours behind him and his stomach rebelled at eating a lunch bigger than Thanksgiving dinner. "The only problem with the food is the quantity."

She tasted the coleslaw and grinned. It was sweet and cold with the right amount of zing. "If there isn't enough, we can always order more."

"More?" Reece groaned. "Are you out of your mind?"

Tennie's spoonful of applesauce halted in midair. Pricilla had promised it was homemade and chunky and had more snap than a bra strap. "What's your problem now?"

"Look at all this food." His arm swept through the air.

She looked at the crowded table and shrugged her shoulders. "You ordered half of it."

Reece flushed a dull red. He couldn't argue that point. He had indeed ordered half the food. Food he would never have ordered even if he had been hungry. The cheeseburger and fries had the fine sheen of animal grease causing his arteries to harden on sight. The slice of cake contained eight thousand calories and the hot sauce coating the chicken wings gave him heartburn smelling it. He tentatively picked up the cheeseburger and took a bite. It was thick, juicy, and delicious. Why was it that everything that was so bad for you tasted so good?

Tennie watched for a moment as Reece chomped away at his burger. With a shrug of her shoulders she went back to her lunch before it got cold.

Twenty minutes later Pricilla arrived with a doggie bag for Reece and a fresh cup of coffee for herself. She handed Reece the bag and slid her ample body into the booth next to him. "Slide that great-looking tush over, sugar. These old feet aren't as young as they once were."

Tennie glanced at Reece's expression and had to

turn her chuckle into a cough. The man looked positively ready to murder someone and she was probably the most likely person.

Pricilla glanced questioningly at Reece and then at Tennie. "What's his problem?"

It took all of Tennie's willpower but she kept a straight face. "He's shy."

Pricilla nudged Reece with an elbow. "All you have to do, sugar, is say you aren't interested and I won't keep bothering you. I heard that the Grizzly's Revenge is filled to the rafters with all kinds of good-looking Montgomerys." She patted the swirl of cotton candy perched on top of her head and grinned at Tennie. "The way Tina, one of the Grizzly's housekeepers, tells it there are Montgomerys of every shape, size, and age."

Tennie returned her grin. Setting Pricilla loose on some of the more stuffy Montgomerys would be an interesting sight. "Yes, ma'am. We have them from eighty-six clear on down to three weeks old."

Pricilla's eyes sparkled with interest. "I was hoping for somewhere in the middle. Old Tailpipe"—she quickly crossed herself—"bless his poor departed soul, was getting a tad rusty." She winked at Tennie. "If you know what I mean."

Before Tennie could respond, Reece broke into the conversation. "Speaking of Tailpipe"—both ladies turned toward him—"how did you two meet?"

Pricilla chuckled and took a sip of her coffee. "This is Little Lincoln, Nevada, not L.A. Everyone knows everyone else's business in Little Lincoln. You can't rightly cuss without everyone else knowing it."

"Were you born and raised here?" Tennie asked.

"Nope. I was born in Atlanta, moved to sunny California when I was sixteen, starred in a few of them picture shows, met and married Ralph back in '56, and moved here."

"Why Little Lincoln?"

"Ralph had family here."

"He doesn't anymore?" Reece asked.

"He's got two sisters still living here, Henrietta and Fanny."

There was such loathing and disgust in the way she had said their names, that Tennie couldn't help asking, "I gather there's some family friction there."

"Friction, hell, it's down-and-out war."

"Anything to do with Tailpipe and your alleged relationship with him?" Tennie questioned.

"Naw, it goes back farther than that. Both my sisters-in-law liked Tailpipe." She drank the rest of her coffee. "Fanny used to have her car serviced by Tailpipe a couple of times a month." She stared into the empty cup. "Everyone in Little Lincoln liked Tailpipe, so I can't see anyone here offing him." Tears filled her eyes and she sniffled delicately. "That's why it had to be Colorado. Number one, he's an outsider, and number two, I heard he was kinda hot for Emma Sue."

Reece glanced at Tennie. He *knew* this was all an act by Pricilla and that no one actually died, but damn, she was good. He pulled a couple of napkins out of the dispenser and handed them to her. "I'm sorry for asking this Pricilla, but were you and Tailpipe having an affair?"

Tennie glared at Reece. The man had no couth. Couldn't he see how upset she was? She reached out and gently patted one of Pricilla's trembling hands. "It's okay, Pricilla, you don't have to answer him."

Pricilla lightly dabbed at her tears and blew her nose. "It's okay. I'm sure you won't be the only ones asking. Tailpipe and I had a very special relationship. Some people might call it an affair, but I prefer to call it an understanding."

"Does that mean you were sleeping—" Reece yelped as Tennie's foot found his shin for the second time.

"Ignore him, Pricilla," Tennie said as she glared at Reece. "Some men are a little insensitive."

Pricilla lightly patted Tennie's hand. "It's okay, sweetie. I've been through it all with the police and the entire town knows every detail by now." She turned toward Reece and slowly smiled. "Do you want to know if Tailpipe and me were doing *the wild thing*?"

Reece swallowed hard at the vision of how many senior citizens were rushed to emergency rooms every year because of *the wild thing*. The hamburger he had just eaten turned over twice in his stomach. "Were you and Tailpipe doing . . ." He couldn't bring himself to call it *the wild thing*. "I mean, were you having an affair?"

"Yes." She raised her empty cup at a passing waitress, who immediately filled it. "Thanks, Gloria."

Tennie glanced at Reece, who shrugged his shoulders. Pricilla had confirmed what the whole town had been saying. "What was your husband's reaction when he found out?" asked Tennie.

"Ralph knew about"—she glanced at Reece and smiled—"the affair before it even started."

"Didn't he try to stop it?" Reece asked.

"Lord no. He understood completely and gave me his blessing years ago."

"Years?" Reece shuddered in astonishment.

"Oh, I see." Pricilla laughed at the shocked expressions on Tennie's and Reece's faces. "You both thought this was something new." She squeezed Tennie's hand and shook her head. "Tailpipe and me go back for years." Her expression grew pensive at some distant memories. "Over six years to be exact."

Reece looked doubtful. "Ralph knew about it all that time?"

"Hell, sugar, it was his idea."

Tennie saw Reece's expression of disbelief. "Pricilla, not that I doubt you, but why would your husband suggest that you have an affair?"

Pricilla tapped her inch-long shocking pink nails against the cup. "It's kind of personal."

"Personal?" questioned Reece. The woman admitted she was doing *the wild thing* with the garage mechanic for six years without batting an eye. What in the world would she possibly consider personal?

"I might as well tell you, I'm sure you're going to find out anyway. The police already know and I'm sure old Fisher has spread it all over town by now."

"Who's Fisher?" Tennie asked.

"One of Little Lincoln's finest. He's about five-seven tall and round. We call him Hoover behind his back because he seems to suck the food right off his plate."

Reece chuckled at the adept description. He had met Officer Fisher at the lodge last night. "If you would have been paying more attention to your surroundings instead of Officer Altman last night, Tennie, you would have met him."

Tennie glared at Reece. "I believe we are being sidetracked. Pricilla was about to tell us what Officer Fisher knows."

"Oh my." Pricilla sighed. "When I met Ralph in California, it was love at first sight. The first time he took me to bed we didn't get out of it for a week. It was pure romance." A heated flush swept up her cheeks at the memories. "Ralph had stamina. He could go on for hours and—"

"We get the picture," Reece managed to say.

"Yes, well." Pricilla fanned herself with a paper napkin. "Everything was hunky-dory until about eight years ago."

"What happened?" Tennie asked.

"Henrietta and Stan's bloodthirsty, miserable, thieving pack of geese is what happened."

Tennie and Reece exchanged glances. "You lost us somewhere."

"Henrietta, Ralph's sister, and her husband have about a dozen pet geese. They're filthy animals that chase you and honk day and night. Their entire front yard is covered with white droppings and the neighbors complain constantly, but do you think they care?" Pricilla waved her hand as her voice rose. "No. They dote on those stupid birds like they were their children for cripes sakes. You mark my words, one day I'm going over there and use those overgrown chickens for target practice and then I'm serving goose for Christmas dinner to the entire town of Little Lincoln."

"Calm down, Pricilla." Tennie smiled at a few of the customers who were looking their way. "We understand about the geese, but what do they have to do with your love life?"

"About eight years ago we went over there one night, it was Stan's birthday. Back then we were still trying to give the appearance of being a family. After Stan blew out the candles I remembered that I had left his present on the front seat of the car. Ralph went outside to get it. That's when it happened."

"What?"

"Those savages attacked my poor Ralph." Tears filled her eyes and she frantically dabbed at them before they could ruin her makeup.

"The geese?" Reece asked.

"Yes, those spawn of Satan. Alfred Hitchcock used the wrong members of the bird family when he made that movie. He should have used geese. They were all over my poor Ralphie. Poking and biting and hissing and honking." A violent shudder shook her body. "It was just terrible. Ralph was screaming something dreadful. I picked up a broom that was on the front porch and I started swinging and the feathers started flying. Henrietta started shrieking at me to stop that I was hurting her babies. By the time it was all over, Ralph was impotent and Henrietta had enough feathers to stuff a comforter."

Tennie's eyes stared unblinkingly at Pricilla. She had no idea what to say. Reece turned three shades of pale and protectively dropped his hands to his lap. "You mean to say Ralph can't . . ." He was at a loss for words.

"Nothing. Zip." Pricilla sighed dramatically and clarified, "His puffer won't puff."

Reece and Tennie sat in silence as Pricilla backed out her Caddy, waved cheerfully, and drove away. The parking lot at Sadie's was filling up with the noon rush but they didn't leave. Reece watched the assortment of customers that Sadie's drew. "Well, what do you think?"

Tennie dug through her purse, looking for a stick of gum. "About what?" She unearthed an old pack of breath mints, threw the top one away, because it was turning a funny shade of blue, and offered one to Reece.

He turned, saw the extended roll of mints, and took one. "Thanks." He popped it into his mouth. "I don't think Ralph did it."

"How can you say that without meeting him?"

"I don't think the man would have given his wife permission to have an affair, wait six years, and then kill her lover."

Tennie thought for a moment. "True, but maybe Pricilla decided to leave Ralph for Tailpipe after all."

"She didn't seem too broken up about Tailpipe's early exit from life."

"True." She watched as Jake Altman pulled up in front of Sadie's and gallantly escorted both North and South Carolina into the diner. "I still think we should leave both Pricilla and Ralph on the suspect list."

"What about Henrietta or Stan?"

"I think we should go talk to them and Ralph. There's one other name I want to add to our list."

"Who's that?"

Tennie chuckled and shook her head. "You mean the great detective didn't pick up on it?"

Reece frowned. "What are you talking about?"

She grinned and placed her sunglasses on the tip of her nose. Her gaze fairly danced with excitement as she looked over the dark lenses at him. "Ralph's sister, Fanny." She slowly pushed the glasses up with her finger.

"What about her?"

"Didn't you hear Pricilla? Fanny took her car into Tailpipe's a couple of times a month."

"Maybe it's a lemon."

"And maybe it wasn't only her car he was servicing."

Reece started the Jeep. "I think you have been talking to Pricilla too long." He jammed the gear shift into reverse and backed out of the space. "There is one thing you seem to be forgetting."

"And that is?"

"Tailpipe is a fictitious character. He never was and never will be real. He wasn't murdered because he was never alive." Reece's voice rose in irritation. "So why do you insist on giving him more action than Mel Gibson on a bad hair day?"

FIVE

Reece parked the Jeep a half block away from the police station in downtown Little Lincoln. He silently got out and glared at the smirking woman emerging from her side of the Jeep. It was a toss up between throttling her or kissing her senseless. Kissing her was winning, hands down. Tennie had given the word *control* a new meaning. How dare she insinuate that he was jealous of a fictitious character, let alone a dead one, for getting more action.

"You better get that scowl off your face before we go in," said Tennie. She briskly marched along the sidewalk. "If Colorado sees you looking like that he will tell Indy we're fighting. Then we'll have to sit through a lecture on getting along and family."

"We're not fighting." He took her elbow and steered her into an alley beside the post office. "In fact I'd say we get along amazingly well."

Tennie glanced up into Reece's eyes. They were

dark, intense, and hungry. Her mouth went dry and she tried to moisten her lips with the tip of her tongue. "Since when?"

Reece captured her chin with the gentlest of touches. His thumb softly stroked her lower lip. "Would you like me to show you how well we could get along?"

She teased his thumb with her teeth and closed her eyes. "No." They definitely shouldn't be doing this. The dangerous ground they were standing on felt entirely too good for her peace of mind.

Reece sucked in his breath as her teeth lightly nipped at his thumb. Need shot through his blood to lay thick and heavy in his loins. "Your words say one thing, but your actions are doing the opposite." He tenderly removed her sunglasses and gazed into her desire-filled eyes. "What is it you really want, Tennie?"

Her chilled fingers caressed his warm cheek. "Sometimes what we want isn't good for us."

"And sometimes it is." He slowly lowered his head and kissed her.

Tennie responded to the sweetness of his kiss. The chill of the April morning turned into a blistering July afternoon as Reece deepened the kiss. Lips fused and tongues danced. His body hardened with quickening desires while hers softened and pressed more closely to his strength.

Reece kissed her once more, deeper than before. The kiss went past merely physical, it touched his soul.

If the exquisite sigh Tennie made was any indication, it touched hers too. He reluctantly broke the kiss and gazed down into her radiant face. She had felt it too. The connection went past the ordinary and crashed right into unique. Whatever was happening between them didn't happen every day. He noticed the confusion edging into her expression and the caution that was lightly pulling at her lower lip. He wanted to kiss her fears away, but this wasn't the time or the place. He tenderly brushed back a wisp of golden blond hair that had been pulled from her ponytail by the wind. "We're here."

Tennie glanced around the neat alley in confusion. "Where is here?"

Reece slowly lifted his hand and pointed to a sign hanging above a newly painted door next to them. It read POLICE DEPARTMENT.

Tennie read the sign and flushed down to her toes. It had to be a first. Reece had her so confused, she didn't even know where they were or where they were heading. How was she ever going to solve the murder if she couldn't remember what she was doing? She hastily straightened her coat, shifted the weight of her purse, and opened the door. "Right. Uncle Colorado."

Reece stood where he was in wonder. Tennessee Montgomery was completely befuddled, and he had done it to her. More accurately his kisses had done it to her, but who cared? All he had to do now was kiss her for the next ten years straight and they might have a chance.

Tennie glanced back over her shoulder at the grinning Reece. "Are you coming?"

He snapped out of his daze and quickly followed her into the police station before she changed her mind and slammed the door in his face.

Four hours later Tennie found herself sitting on an isolated outcrop of rocks, staring at the wonder of nature called the Sierras. After leaving the crowded police station she asked Reece to drive back to the lodge. Practically every member of her family had been jammed into the tiny station, badgering Officer Fisher and drilling poor locked-up Colorado. When Tailpipe's widow, Emma Sue, arrived to deliver Colorado his lunch, total pandemonium had broken out. Tennie and Reece had decided instead of combating the family and a stubborn Colorado, they would leave and try again later. Only problem was, most of the family had followed them back to the inn. They had been cornered in the lounge for fifteen minutes by Aunt Florida and Aunt Maine. When Uncle Utah joined them, Tennie had slipped out of the lodge and headed for the nearest path into the wilderness. After hiking for twenty minutes she had found the perfect place to rest and think.

Everything seemed to be happening at once. The list of murder suspects was ballooning out of control, Colorado was totally smitten with the new widow, Emma Sue, and poor Tailpipe wasn't even cold in the ground yet. Pricilla was looking to vamp the entire town of Little Lincoln, Ralph was suffering a goose phobia, and where did the elusive Fanny fit in the murder? The more she thought, the greater the number of questions she had.

Tennie sighed softly. All this was only a game, a game that two weeks ago she had her heart set on winning at any cost. Now she didn't care a dippity-do about winning or even solving the mystery. The reason she didn't care anymore could be answered with two words, Reece Carpenter.

The man was a walking menace to her peace of mind. For two years now she had been avoiding her own family just to place some distance between Reece and herself. It was one thing to secretly fantasize about him while being over a thousand miles away, it was quite another story with him being in the same room. So what happened this year? For some reason he shows up at the reunion all smiles and kisses. Whatever attraction she felt for Reece was beside the point, it could never work out. They were too different in too many areas, but more importantly they were the same in others.

She knew she bordered on being a slob while Reece scaled the walls of compulsive neatness. It wasn't that she wanted to be a slob, but more important things always demanded her time. Who wanted to scrub the bathroom floor, or clean out a closet, when there were criminals to be caught and cases to be solved? This morning when she heard Reece leave his room for breakfast, she'd opened their connecting door and confirmed her fears. Reece's room was immaculate. Clothes were neatly hung in the closet, precisely one inch apart and not one drop of shaving scum was splattered in the sink. She had returned to her room, gone through a pile of her clothes that had made it to the top of the bureau instead of inside it, found and pulled on a pair of faded jeans and a baggy sweatshirt.

Tennie gazed out over the mountains and smiled as a huge bird floated on the wind. She pulled up her knees and wrapped her arms around them. The late afternoon was turning chilly. She plopped her chin down onto her knees.

If Reece and she could somehow conquer this opposites-attract rule, it still wouldn't work. They were too much alike in their careers. Both wanted to be the best, and by the simple definition of the word, only one could be the best. They both wanted to be number one. Any relationship she could form with Reece would be sliced to ribbons by competitiveness. They would fight over clients, over motives, over investigating techniques. The clash of the Titans would seem like a playground scuffle by the time they were through with each other.

Maybe she was thinking way ahead of herself. After all, they had only kissed three times. But she knew where those kisses were heading, straight to her heart and into her bed. It was born and bred into her to think ahead, to look systematically at a sequence of events, and to know exactly what went wrong. It was the curse of being a great detective.

She groaned and wondered when she had become so pessimistic? She followed the graceful glide of another hawk as he searched for his dinner. She was so deep in concentration following the hawk that she nearly toppled over when a twig snapped nearby. She quickly turned around and stared at Reece standing less than three feet away. "Lord, couldn't you have knocked or something?"

Reece chuckled and glanced around him. Not a door in sight. "Sorry, I didn't mean to startle you." He breathed deeply and gazed out over the mountains. "I've been standing here for about five minutes."

"Why didn't you say something?" She didn't like the idea of Reece standing there staring at her.

"I didn't want to disturb you." He gestured to the outcrop of rocks she was sitting on. "May I?"

"It's a free country." Hopefully he'd take the hint and leave her alone before she did something incredibly stupid, like kiss him again. She turned her attention back to one of the mountains in the distance.

Reece slowly sat down, leaving a good twelve inches of rock between them. Tennie was acting stranger than usual. Was she regretting their kisses? Maybe she was willing to face the wrath of Indy and dissolve their partnership. Hell, she might even be thinking about heading back to Iowa. He picked up a small pebble and started to roll it between his fingers. "So what do you think?"

"About what?"

"Colorado and Emma Sue." He glanced at her expression, trying to figure out exactly where her mind had been. Wherever it was, it hadn't been on the investigation. "I think they make a cute couple."

"I have to agree with you on that." She had spent her entire life observing her uncles, imitating them, and loving them. Colorado was the oldest, had a heart of gold, loved working in his garden back in California, and was the world's worst actor. Colorado hadn't been acting when Emma Sue showed up at the police station bringing him lunch. His affection had been real, and if Emma Sue's expression was anything to go by, so was hers. "Even if Emma Sue's totally smitten with Colorado, it still seems odd that she cooks his meals and delivers them to the jail. After all, the man is behind bars for the murder of her husband."

"Maybe they conspired together to take Tailpipe out of the picture."

"Leave it to my family to stage a crime of passion when the gentleman is so ancient." She shook her head, causing her ponytail to swish from side to side catching the late-afternoon sun. "Your theory might have some merit, except for one thing—I've known Colorado all my life. Even if, and that's a big if, he thought about removing Tailpipe from the scene, he would do it in a more inventive way than smashing him. Colorado was one of the best. I'm sure he could come up with a way to eliminate his sweetie's husband without anyone ever suspecting foul play."

"You're probably right." He studied the way the sun gleamed through her hair. "Colorado would be too smart to allow someone to place him near the crime scene. Did you happen to hear who saw him there, anyway?"

"Stan Marino, who happens to be Henrietta's husband, told Officer Fisher he saw Colorado right outside the garage about ten o'clock on the morning of the murder."

"The autopsy report said that death occurred between nine-thirty and ten."

"The police are figuring the time of death to be nine forty-eight," said Tennie. "Tailpipe's watch had stopped at that time when it was crushed." She saw Reece shudder and grinned. Her family loved throwing a little gore into their fictional crimes. Their logic was that there weren't too many murders that didn't contain some type of gore. They had stayed away from using physical evidence during the reunions because of the small children who attended. Last year she had heard Pinky and Georgia discussing the possibilities of having an "Adult's Only" get-together one year. Tennie shivered at the possibilities her family could come up with then. There would be corpses littering the lobbies of the best hotels across America. "Did you happen to hear during all that confusion why Colorado was in Little Lincoln to begin with?"

"Fishing trip. The Roaring River has some of the best trout fishing in North America. Colorado wanted to try his hand at it."

"Did he catch anything?"

"From all appearances, only Emma Sue and a possible life sentence."

"Some partner you are."

"I did find out one interesting fact."

"What's that?"

"Colorado was renting a cabin near the river."

"So?"

"Guess who owns the cabin he was renting?" Reece tossed a pebble into the air and caught it. "Emma Sue's father."

"He has to be over ninety!"

"He's ninety-seven and living in a nursing home in Wellington. Emma Sue rents out the cabin to help pay for some of his medical bills."

"That must be how she and Colorado met."

"Looks that way." Reece gave Tennie a tender smile and gently cupped her cheek. "Does that make me a better partner?"

She leaned into the warmth of his palm and teased him. "You're the best partner I ever had."

Reece wrapped his arms around her. "I'm the only partner you ever had. A Montgomery always works alone." He carefully pulled her closer and lightly brushed a kiss across her mouth.

Tennie pulled back and turned her head away. She didn't want Reece to see the hurt in her eyes. He had been right, a Montgomery always worked alone. For a moment there it felt so good just to sit with Reece and discuss the case that she had forgotten it was all temporary. In a matter of days Reece would be heading back to sunny California, and she would be packing her bags and going home to Iowa. Only a fool went looking for heartache.

He followed Tennie's gaze. She seemed totally hypnotized by a bird soaring in the distance. "What are you thinking about?"

Tennie kept her gaze pinned on the hawk. There was no way she was telling him the truth. "I was thinking about what that hawk was going to have for dinner."

Reece shaded his eyes and studied the bird. "It's a golden eagle and you don't have to worry."

The man was impossible. He even knew it wasn't a hawk just by looking at it. "I don't?"

"I won't let him carry you off." His lips curved in a sensual smile that promised heaven. "We already have dinner plans."

Tennie fought down the desire tightening her throat and the wild beating of her heart. She knew it was all wrong, but she wanted him anyway. "We do?"

"Most definitely." His hungry gaze feasted on her trembling lower lip. He could think of a thousand different ways he would love to taste her. With a reluctant sigh he said, "We've been asked to join Indy and Pinky for dinner."

Tennie shifted restlessly in her chair and studied her grandmother. She looked much better tonight.

Her cheeks held a touch of color and her appetite had improved greatly. So why was she feeling something wasn't quite right? The dining room was packed with Montgomerys. Conversations were buzzing, dinnerware was clanging. All in all it looked like a typical Montgomery reunion. Total chaos.

Reece leaned closer to her ear and whispered, "Are you all right?"

"Yes, why?"

"Because ever since you sat down you seem to have ants in your pants or something."

Tennie noticed her grandparents' glances and forced a pleasant smile. All she wanted to do was get out of there. Sitting through dinner acting like Reece and she were the greatest partners since Laurel and Hardy was stretching her nerves. Every time she answered one of her grandparents' questions concerning the investigation, Reece always added a few opinions of his own. It wouldn't have been too bad, but all his opinions contradicted hers. Their small list of suspects had mushroomed out of control during dinner. Every time she mentioned who was on the list, Reece would add another suspect to be investigated. Tennie, being Tennie, couldn't allow him to have the last word, so she added another suspect, which made Reece bring up another name, causing her to add another name. So the list grew and grew.

Her cheeks hurt from pleasantly smiling, her teeth ached from being ground together, and she was freezing her tush off. If she never saw another pair of French-cut panties, it would be too soon. The deep purple silky dress she was wearing was entirely wrong for the Grizzly's Revenge. Even with its sophisticated matching jacket it didn't offer one ounce of warmth. When she had bought the dress, she had visualized wearing it on some patio on Maui, sipping iced drinks with bright little umbrellas sticking out of their tops. Not in some rustic lodge constructed out of logs and with a heating system that was older than the Constitution. She leaned closer to Reece and whispered back, "It's freezing in here."

Reece who had been secretly studying the enticing view provided by her low-cut dress whole-heartedly disagreed. As far as he was concerned someone should open a window or two. "Tsk, tsk, Tennie. Are you wearing those French panties again?"

Tennie shifted in her chair and glanced at her grandparents to make sure they couldn't hear. They seemed to be totally engrossed in their own conversation. "Of course I am. The nice thick cotton ones with 'Friday' stitched across the rear just didn't go with the outfit."

Reece started to choke as a mouthful of coffee went down the wrong way. Tennie continued to smile pleasantly.

"Reece, are you all right?" Pinky cried. Her aged hands fluttered with a napkin for an instant.

"Fine, fine," Reece said as soon as he could get his breath back. "It just went down the wrong way." He shot a quick scowl at Tennie. He knew he had deserved that comment, but it still had caught him by surprise. He focused on the teasing light dancing in her eyes, causing them to appear more green than hazel, and the seductive curve of her lower lip.

"Are you ready to order dessert?" asked their waitress who had appeared next to the table.

Indy looked regretfully at Pinky and squeezed her hand. "Could we have a small plate of fruit?"

Tennie shook her head. She couldn't handle the cold any longer. More than a piece of cheesecake she wanted her nice warm sweatpants—and to be away from Reece. "I think I'll pass on dessert if you don't mind, Grandmom. It's been a long day and I still have a bunch of stuff to sort through in my mind before I can call it a night." Like all the great Montgomerys before her, Tennie never took notes. Everything was stored in her memory. With the way her mind was working lately it was going to take a miracle to solve this case.

Reece looked at the waitress and said, "I think I'll pass too."

"I'm heading on up now." Tennie tenderly kissed her grandparents. "Take care and I'll see you at breakfast."

Reece watched her leave. The deep purple of her dress shimmered and glistened in the low light of the dining room. Her hips swayed gently as she threaded her way through the tables, dropping a word here and there as she went. Visions of French-cut panties, silk stockings, and lacy garters caused an eruption of heat low in his body. He remembered the way she had melted in his arms outside the police station and groaned.

"Reece?"

He turned around fast and faced the concerned look on Indy's face. "Yes, sir."

"Indy, boy, Indy." He took a sip of his coffee. "Is everything all right between you and Tennie?"

"In regard to what, sir . . . I mean, Indy?" Surely the desire he felt for Indy's precious granddaughter wasn't that obvious.

Indy cocked a white eyebrow. "I was referring to your partnership."

Reece swallowed hard. "It's going as well as can be expected."

"Meaning?"

He respected Indy too much to lie to him. "Meaning, sir, she's a Montgomery."

Indy and Pinky broke out laughing. "Say no more, we both understand. Why don't you stop by the kitchen and make up a tray of cheesecake and coffee and take it up to Tennie. I'm sure you both have a lot to discuss concerning this case. By the sounds of things over dinner you have your work cut out for you."

Reece stood up. "That's an excellent idea." He tenderly bent down and kissed Pinky's cheek. "Did I ever tell you how much I love having you as a grandmother?"

Pinky's face flooded with the soft rose of her blush. "The feeling is mutual, Reece." She patted his cheek.

"Now get going. There's a murderer on the loose and my dear brother-in-law is rotting away in jail."

Indy and Pinky watched as Reece left the room. They both turned to each other and grinned. Indy bowed his head in admiration and said, "Excellent move, my love. Simply brilliant." He raised his hand and called the waitress over. "Could we please change our dessert order to two slices of cheesecake and two glasses of white wine." He winked at Pinky. "I think this calls for a celebration."

SIX

Tennie glared at the door of her hotel room. Someone was knocking on it. She dropped the pile of clothes she had been searching through on the bed and stormed over to the door. She had been back in her room for ten minutes and still hadn't found her gray sweat suit. Her arms, legs, back—oh hell, her entire body was freezing and her feet felt like solid blocks of ice. She yanked open the door and glared at Reece. "What do you want?"

Reece's smile only faltered for a moment. "I've brought a peace offering."

"I didn't realize we were fighting." She looked at the two pieces of cheesecake smothered in cherries and her mouth started to water.

"We're not." He shifted the tray so the enticing aroma floating out of the coffeepot teased her senses. "I was hoping to talk you into discussing the case some more tonight."

Tennie opened the door farther and stepped back. "Well, maybe for a little while." Reece walked into the room and had to wait until Tennie removed the junk piled on the small table before setting down the tray. "Pour me a cup of coffee while I get changed. If that heater doesn't start spitting out heat soon, I'm calling down to complain."

He didn't feel cold, but Tennie was known to have that effect on him. "Why don't you change and I'll check it."

Tennie sighed as she looked through the clothes piled on top of the bureau. Frustrated, she looked in the last place she could think of.

Reece stopped in the middle of pouring her coffee as Tennie knelt on the floor and looked under the bed. An enticing view of her bottom bounced before his eyes. A groan of despair stuck in his throat. How was he supposed to concentrate on the case when visions of purple heart-shaped bottoms danced in his mind?

"Eureka! Found it!" Tennie shouted as her bottom wiggled backward and she stood up clutching the rumpled sweat suit.

"You lost your clothes?"

"Nope, just misplaced them." Tennie slipped off the light jacket that matched the dress and hooked it over the doorknob.

Reece's breath joined the groan caught in his throat. Tennie's dress had no back. Creamy satin skin from the base of her neck to the tempting small of her back enthralled his senses. "I can see now why you were cold."

Tennie started to search through the pile of clothes again. *Don't tell me I forgot to pack more socks!* "What?" Her hand slid to the back of her dress. "Oh, the dress. Don't tell me. I've already figured it wasn't the smartest choice to pack for this trip."

"No, no," he hurriedly reassured her. "It's gorgeous." He saw Tennie raise a delicate brow. "What I meant was you're gorgeous in it." He liked the way her cheeks turned pink. "Then again you look gorgeous in anything." The pink turned to a brilliant red. "I hope you got it at a half-price sale."

"Why?"

Reece grinned. "Because it's only half there."

Tennie threw a hairbrush at him and marched into the bathroom.

He caught the brush and laughed at the closed door. Still shaking his head over her temperament he walked over to the thermostat and gave it a few taps. Tennie had it turned up to eighty degrees but it was reading the room temperature at sixty-four. After a few more taps he heard the slight hissing sound of air being forced from the heater. He placed his hands over the heater and grinned. It was hot air.

Tennie emerged from the bathroom, saw Reece rubbing his hands above the heater, and ran across the room. "You did it!" She laid her hands directly on top of the vents and sighed, "Heat." She turned her hands over to warm up the other side. "How did you do it?"

"Just keep tapping your thermostat. There was dust or something in there I guess."

"Thanks, Reece." Her smile was soft and sincere.

He took a step closer and whispered, "You're welcome." The enchanting perfume that had teased him throughout dinner still clung to her skin.

Tennie could feel the dangerous ground they were standing on start to shake. "Reece?"

His fingers played with a wisp of her golden hair that was resting on her shoulder. "Hmmm . . ."

"Can I borrow something?" She had to break this spell before she surrendered to the demands of her body.

"Anything."

"Great." She hurried over to their interconnecting door. It was still unlocked. "Thanks." She flipped on his light switch and bolted into his room.

Reece followed and watched as she opened up the first drawer of the bureau and pulled out a pair of his thick sweatsocks.

Tennie sadly shook her head. "So predictable."

"What is?"

She glanced back over her shoulder and studied the bemused expression on his face. "I bet if I pull open the drawer next to the one I just opened, your underwear would be in it." She opened the drawer and looked at the neat stack of white briefs. "The hardest question that I had to answer was, would you keep your socks in the right-hand drawer, or the left?"

Reece frowned. He didn't know if he liked being

called predictable by Tennie. "What made you choose the left side?"

Tennie sat down on the edge of Reece's bed and yanked his thick white socks over her frozen piggies. "Modesty."

"Modesty?"

"You're right-handed, so I would assume you open drawers with your right hand. Being modest you would naturally reach for the drawer containing your skivvies first." She yanked on the second sock. "By the way your taste in men's underwear is also predictable." She stood up and passed him to get back into her room.

Now he knew he didn't like being called predictable. "There's nothing wrong with my taste in underwear. I've been wearing that brand since the day I was potty trained."

Tennie grinned over her shoulder. "Bingo!"

Reece walked into his room and closed both drawers that she had left open before following her over to the coffee he had poured. He sat down in the empty chair, not feeling gracious enough to clear the other chair of the junk she had dumped there. He nodded toward her cup. "Drink up before it gets cold."

She took a sip and looked up in surprise. "You remembered how I took it."

"Three packets of sugar and hold the cream." She was the only woman alive who would put three whole packets of sugar into every cup of coffee she drank and not worry about the calories. "I still haven't figured out why you don't weigh two hundred pounds."

"I beg your pardon?" She dumped the junk from the chair onto the floor and sat down. She propped her feet up onto the heater and wiggled her toes.

"It must be your metabolism or something."

Tennie picked up the plate of cheesecake and took a bite. "Touchy subject, Reece. Never talk about a woman's weight or her age." She took another bite. "I thought you came here to discuss the case."

"Yes, well . . ."

"Well, what?"

He poked the tip of his cake with the fork. "I think our list of suspects got out of hand during dinner."

Tennie continued to eat. "What gave you the first clue?"

"When you suggested the loan officer at Little Lincoln National Bank."

"I only suggested him because of the threatening letters he had been sending Tailpipe. He might have considered the advantages and decided it was good business to knock Tailpipe off and collect the outstanding balance from his life insurance. It would be a lot faster than waiting for him to make good on the payments."

"How do you know Tailpipe had any life insurance?"

"I called the bank." She put down the empty plate and cup and slumped farther into the chair. Warmth had finally returned to her body.

"How much life insurance did he have?" By the looks of the garage, Reece hadn't considered money as a motive. It just went to show how Tennie had messed up his mind. Eighty percent of all homicides were motivated by greed or passion.

"Zippo." She wiggled her toes some more. "The life insurance he was carrying only covered the outstanding balance of the loan at the time of his death. From what Mr. Johnson, at the bank, tells me, Tailpipe had another policy but Emma Sue would have to have buried him in an old cardboard box for the check to cover the funeral expenses."

"No other assets?"

"He and Emma Sue paid off their mortgage on a small, but plain, two-bedroom rancher on Mary Todd Avenue about four years ago. That's what he used for collateral on the loan he acquired from Little Lincoln National Bank."

"How big a loan was it?"

"Five thousand."

"Gee." Reece gazed at Tennie and smiled. She looked half asleep in the chair. Her eyes were closed and she seemed to be basking in the heat pouring from the heater. She reminded him of a golden-haired cat all content after a big meal. His fingers itched to tenderly stroke her and listen to her purr. "What was the loan for?"

Tennie peeked out from below lowered lashes and dropped her bombshell. "Improvements on the garage."

Reece sputtered. "How long ago did he take out the loan?"

"Four months ago." She smiled at Reece's reaction and chalked one up for her side. "Oh, and he never made one payment to the bank."

"Nothing in four months?"

"Nothing." She continued to smile. Life was beginning to take a turn for the better. She had Reece frustrated at himself for not thinking of the bank first.

"Where's the money? He obviously didn't sink one dime into the garage." Reece frowned. Tennie might look like some well-satisfied cat, but she was apparently as cunning as a fox. "Did he have any in a savings account?"

"Emma Sue and he had joint savings and checking accounts. There was only about three thousand in the savings, and a grand total of one hundred and fifty in the checking. Apparently they were living on her social security and what little he made at the garage."

"So where's the five grand?"

"Don't know yet." She recrossed her ankles and sighed. "I'm working on it."

"Why didn't you tell me you were going to call the bank?" He didn't like the idea that she had discovered the best lead so far.

"Why didn't you tell me you were going back into town before dinner?" Her gaze turned rock-hard and her voice was edged with frost. "Want to tell me what Ralph Stone had to say?"

"How did you know I talked to Ralph?"

"Aunt Maine stopped me in the lobby after I left

you at dinner. Her bursitis was acting up and she had to go into town to fill a prescription. Seems she saw you leaving the beer distributor and was concerned as to why we weren't together." She smiled mockingly. "Being the Dynamic Duo and all."

Reece shifted uncomfortably in the chair. "What did you tell her?"

"I could have told her the truth, but it would have found its way back to Pinky and broken her heart, so I lied. I told her that I had cramps and was resting in my room. You, being the perfect gentleman and all, naturally agreed to hold the investigation together and interview a potential suspect."

"What did she say to that?" In his own mind it sounded as phoney as a three-dollar bill. Tennie would never allow something as common as cramps to keep her from an investigation.

"She told me to take vitamin C pills." Tennie lowered her nice and toasty feet and sat up. "Why didn't you tell me you were heading back into town?"

He sighed. Not only had he misled Tennie, but the entire trip had been in vain. Even driving a couple of miles away couldn't put the enticing picture she made sitting on that outcrop of rocks behind him. Her seductive image had stayed with him every mile. "I thought we could use some time apart."

"Meaning?"

Reece stood up and paced to the door and back. Frustrated, he asked, "Do you have any idea what you do to me?"

"Aggravate the hell out of you?"

He tried not to chuckle. "Besides that."

Tennie smiled when she noticed his lips twitching. "The words irritate, frustrate, and terrify come to mind."

Reece stopped his pacing directly in front of her chair. "You think I'm terrified?"

"That another detective would show you up, and a female one no less."

He leaned down and put a hand on each arm of her chair. "That's not the reason you terrify me, Tennie."

"It's not?"

"No." He leaned in closer. "Do you know what I wanted to do this afternoon when I found you sitting on those rocks in the middle of nowhere?"

She saw the hungry gleam that had leapt into his gaze. "If I have to guess, I would say, throw me off the mountain."

"That's your first guess, you have two more."

She knew exactly where this was all heading, but she tried to prevent the inevitable. "You wanted to strangle me?"

"One more guess." His fingers lightly stroked her throat. She had been breathtaking sitting outside in the fading afternoon light. He'd used every ounce of willpower he possessed to resist gathering her into his arms and satisfying the desire that flared every time they were together. This evening at dinner she had been stunningly beautiful and sexy. But now she was gorgeous wearing nothing more than a baggy sweat suit. She looked all comfy and warm. He wanted to sink into that warmth.

His touch seared her skin. The flames dancing from his fingertips matched the ones in his eyes. Her gaze locked onto his lips. "You wanted to kiss me?"

He groaned and closed the remaining distance between them. His breath softly fluttered against her mouth. "I wanted to do more than just kiss you, Tennie." His lips tenderly brushed across hers. "I wanted to lay you down on a bed of soft pine needles and bury myself so far in you that it would take a week before I could find my way back."

She silently cursed the excitement bubbling in her stomach. Reece's words were conjuring up the same images she had been fantasizing about for two years. Images she had always run from. Images she had always felt were better left unexplored. Until now. If there were any reasons why she shouldn't welcome Reece's kisses, she forgot them. Her voice was dreamy soft and filled with wonder. "Really?"

His control snapped. He hauled her up into his arms and crushed her mouth to his.

Tennie raised her arms to encircle his neck and held him close. Heaven. This was what she had been waiting for all her life. It felt so right. She slowly stroked her tongue across his lower lip and smiled as she felt his shuddering response. She gloried in the sensation of being crushed against his chest. Her breasts felt heavy and sensitive. Her nipples pouted and begged for the touch of his hands or the gentle pull of his lips.

Reece moaned as his tongue slipped between her lips. His hands cupped her hips and pulled her closer to his straining body. The taste of Tennessee teased his senses like the intoxicating flavor of golden whiskey, deliciously smooth and sinful. He slanted his mouth more and deepened the kiss.

Tennie matched Reece's dueling tongue stroke for stroke, thrust for thrust. Their desire fed off each other, building ever higher. She pushed her hips slightly forward and felt his manhood, strong and sure behind the denim barrier of his jeans. Reece wanted her as much as she wanted him. She threw back her head and broke the kiss as muscular hands cupped her bottom and brought her fully against his arousal. His feverish mouth skimmed her neck and paused at her rapidly pounding pulse. She cried his name, "Reece?"

He tried to slow his breathing and regain some command over the situation that was spinning out of control faster than a child's top. This was Tennie in his arms, blowing his good intentions straight out the window and into her bed. This was his stepfather's goddaughter. This was the precious granddaughter of Indy and Pinky Montgomery, two of the most fantastic people he had ever met. They had graciously opened their arms, their hearts, and their family and allowed him to enter, and this was how he was repaying their trust. This was Tennie, the woman he wanted more than his next breath. His hands slowly released her and allowed them some breathing space. He nearly lost his resolve as he gently brushed a lingering kiss across her lips. "Tennie?"

She slowly opened her eyes and lowered her hands as her body screamed in protest. She hadn't expected Reece to back off. If the strained look hardening his expression was anything to go by, he wasn't too pleased with the idea himself. His jaw was clenched tighter than Scrooge's wallet and the wild flames dancing in his eyes seemed to burn into her soul. His face was flushed and his breathing was ragged. All in all, Reece gave the appearance of a man very close to the edge. Her fingers nervously toyed with the stretched and frayed hem of her sweatshirt. Curiosity overruled her embarrassment. "Why did you stop?"

"Because if I didn't, I wouldn't have stopped until some time after dawn." He stroked the side of his thumb down the creamy smoothness of her neck and silently cursed at the slight abrasion his roughened jaw had caused. Tennie's skin was extremely delicate and would require him shaving more than once a day. He rubbed at his offending chin. It felt like low-grade sandpaper. "Sorry about that. Next time I'll remember to shave first."

"Next time?" Tennie pressed her hand against her stomach to contain the butterflies fluttering around in there. Hell, they weren't butterflies, they were more like giant whooping cranes, whooping and hollering and raising a storm. The delicious cheesecake she had just eaten shifted over to allow the cranes more dancing room.

"Don't look so surprised, Tennie. There definitely will be a next time." He traced the fullness of her lip with the soft pad of his thumb. "And a next time, and a next time. I can't think of any reason why we would ever have to stop."

"What about eating?"

Reece chuckled. "Leave it to you to think of food."

She grimaced. It wasn't as if she constantly thought of food, it just so happened that one of the huge whooping cranes plopped his butt into the cheesecake. Still confused, she asked, "Why isn't there a *this* time?"

He ran trembling fingers through his hair and took a few steps backward. He needed to put a few good yards between Tennie and his throbbing libido. "I want you to be sure."

"Sure?"

"Yes, sure." He glanced wishfully at the bed. "I'm not talking about a one-night stand, Tennie. One night with you would never be enough."

"What are you suggesting?" She followed his gaze toward the bed and frowned. Between the time when the maid had straightened it this morning and now, she had managed to pile a weekend's worth of clothes at the foot of the bed. Dumping half the contents of her enormous purse over the bed didn't help matters. Even if Reece did decide to take her to bed, they would have to use his or spend ten minutes digging hers out.

He didn't like the frown pulling at her mouth as she gazed at the bed. Tennie was obviously not ready for any declarations of undying affections of love. "I was thinking along the lines of a small commitment first."

"What kind of small commitment?" In the matter of a week he'd be heading back to sunny California and she'd be packing her bags for the return trip to Iowa. As far as she could tell, that didn't leave room for any kind of commitment.

"How about we start with an agreement not to see anyone else during the reunion."

Confused, she asked, "As in dating?"

"Right." That should erase that fretful look off her face. They would take it real slow. He mentally kicked himself as he realized they had about a week left of the reunion. He couldn't afford to go slowly.

"Reece, who exactly would I be dating? In case you haven't put two and two together here, we're at a reunion. A *family* reunion. That means all the men here are my family, present company excluded."

"What about Jake Altman?"

"He's an actor for cripes sake, Reece. He's being paid to divert my attention from the case."

"Is it working?"

"No." She placed both hands on her hips and glared. "You have managed to achieve that feat all by yourself."

"I have?"

"Yes, you have."

Reece grinned. "That's great."

"No, it's not."

"It's not?"

"Reece, in case it slipped your mind, I'm your partner. You are supposed to want me thinking about the case constantly so we can solve it."

He continued to grin as he closed the distance between them. "I don't mind if you spend all your time thinking of me." He gently tucked a lock of her hair behind her ear. "What do you think about when you think of me?" Call it egotistical, but he had less than a week to convince Tennie to take a chance on him.

"Right now?" Her gaze dropped suggestively to his mouth.

He had to clear his throat twice before he could speak. "Yeah."

Her glance shot back up to his eyes. "Homicide."

He smiled, but took a safe step back anyway. "I guess I deserved that."

"And a lot more."

He took another step toward the interconnecting door. "How about if we finish this conversation over breakfast tomorrow morning?"

"I think this conversation is already finished, Reece."

"If you meet me for breakfast at eight o'clock, I'll fill you in on what Ralph Stone had to say."

She studied him as he opened the door and stepped

into his own room. "We were supposed to talk about that tonight."

"Yeah, well, we got sidetracked a little."

"A little?" As far as she was concerned his little sounded like the same little as in a little bit dead.

Reece made a grand showing of looking at his watch. "Will you look at the time! Where has it gone?" If he didn't leave now, he wasn't going to. Tennie looked too tempting. He slowly started to close the door between them. "I'll see you downstairs at eight."

The door was a fraction of an inch from being closed when Tennie's voice stopped it. "Reece?"

He kept the door safely between them. "Yes?"

"Montgomerys don't run from problems or postpone them. They meet them head-on."

"You could end up in a whole lot of trouble that way, Tennie. Carpenters always think before they leap."

"It could be a whole lot of heaven, Reece. Did you ever think of that?"

"Every night, Tennie. Every night." The door softly closed between them.

Tennie stood in the middle of her lonely hotel room and stared at the door he had just closed. She didn't know if she should throw something at it, or smile. Reece had backed off so she could think about making love with him. She turned away from the door and paced over to the windows. What was there to think about? She wanted him, and he wanted her.

They were both mature adults who knew what they were getting into. She glared at the door. It remained closed. Well, maybe she *didn't* know what they'd be getting into.

Reece wasn't interested in her because of the Montgomery name. He was already part of the family. Hell, he even had a chance to legally change his name to Montgomery and had turned it down. Reece wasn't interested in opening up a detective agency with the name Montgomery splashed above the door. His own agency in San Francisco was well established and respected. Whatever reasons Reece wanted her, professional wasn't one of them.

That only left personal. Years ago when she had trusted her instincts with men, Reece would have filled every one of her qualifications for a lover, and had some left over. He was attractive, ambitious, intelligent, and honest. He was a man's man and every woman's fantasy rolled into one. Reece could make a woman think of forever, babies, and growing old together. He was totally wrong for her.

Frustrated at the world and its injustices, Tennie jammed her feet into her sneakers and slipped on her coat. She picked up a mismatched pair of mittens, a yellow woolly hat with a lime-green pom-pom on top, and pocketed her room key. With one regretful glance at the closed interconnecting door, she quietly let herself out of her room. She had always wanted to go tramping through the Sierras in the middle of the night.

SEVEN

"Well I still don't see why you couldn't have had breakfast with me," Reece said. He jammed the Jeep into second and continued down the steep mountain road heading toward town.

"I told you earlier that Aunt Florida needed my opinion on something."

He took his gaze off the road for an instant and glared at Tennie. "What precisely did she need your opinion on? Something concerning the case?"

"It didn't have anything to do with the case." She pulled a Minnesota Twin's baseball hat from her purse and tucked all her flying hair up under it as she put it on her head. It was a perfect morning for driving with the top down. A bit nippy, but the biting wind should keep the conversation down to bare minimum. "It was personal."

Reece slowed the Jeep down until the wind stopped howling and he could hear himself think. He knew the reason Tennie, who hated to be cold, insisted on putting down the top. She was scared to death he was going to mention last night. "What did you say?"

"I said, Aunt Florida needed my opinion on a personal matter."

Reece gave her a look that clearly said she was lying. "Oh, really."

"Yes, really." Tennie turned her collar up against the wind and pulled her freezing hands into the sleeves of her coat. She had left her mittens back in her room. "North and South Carolina are dating the same man."

Reece raised an eyebrow, but continued to drive slowly. "Do they know the other one is dating him too?"

"Yes. Aunt Florida says they seem very comfortable with the relationship. She's the one who is having a problem with it."

"I can imagine." He gently braked for a sharp turn in the road. "It must be hard having a family get-together. Which one gets to invite her fellow?"

"Oh, they're not dating him separately."

"They're not?" asked Reece confused.

"No, that's not Florida's problem. Whenever they go out it's a threesome."

Reece slammed on the brakes and stared at Tennie. "You mean he dates both of them at the same time?"

"Yep. Florida's afraid this will drive a wedge between the girls." She frowned at the thought. "You know how the girls finish each other's sentences all the time. Suppose they do have a falling-out, do you think they would be able to hold a conversation?"

"Maybe it's a good thing if someone pulls them apart a little. You know, let them become individuals." He noticed Tennie's thoughtful expression. "How long have they been dating this two-timing Romeo?"

"Since yesterday."

"Yesterday!" Reece cried. "Who?"

"Jake the Fake Altman."

Reece relaxed. "Maybe he's just diverting them the way you think he's being paid to divert you?"

"North and South Carolina couldn't win at a game of Clue if they were the only ones playing. I love them dearly, Reece, but face it, they were gypped on their share of the Montgomerys' genes. Jake would have picked up on that and not bothered to waste his acting skills. Besides, why would he try to divert them in a different way from the one he used on me?"

"What do you mean?"

"He took them to lunch yesterday and then last night he showed up here with two bouquets of flowers and took them both dancing up at some fancy place in Wellington."

Reece started their journey again. "The man either has more stamina than I gave him credit for, or he has a fetish for twins, or he's totally insane."

"Or . . ." Tennie gazed thoughtfully out the side window.

"Or what?"

"Maybe he's smarter than we think. Suppose he's trying to throw us off the track of the killer?"

"By dating North and South Carolina?"

Tennie hugged herself tighter as the wind blew harder, and wished she had never convinced Reece to put down the top. "Stranger things have happened during our family reunions, Reece."

Reece thought about Jake and his courting hormones the rest of the way into Little Lincoln. That meant either Jake had killed Tailpipe or he was covering for the real killer. Now why would Jake want to kill a seventy-two-year-old mechanic? He turned the Jeep down Main Street and past Tailpipe's garage.

"Where are we going?" Tennie asked. "Isn't Fanny's house back that way?" She pointed over her shoulder and to the left.

"I wanted to check out something first." Last night, around three in the morning, it occurred to him that he was never going to get the chance to have Tennie to himself unless he planned it that way. Between the mystery and her family something was always demanding her attention. All he wanted was a couple of hours of Tennie's undivided attention and company. He didn't want pushy aunts, vamping waitresses, or bogus cops popping up every few minutes. If kidnapping her was the only way to achieve his goal, so be it. He wasn't going to have another year go by comparing every woman to Tennie; he wanted the real thing.

Reece turned the Jeep onto a dirt road and headed deeper into the woods. He hoped the manager of the inn knew what he was talking about when he claimed *Big View* was the most secluded and romantic spot this side of Wellington. "The Roaring River is just about a mile in front of us."

"Oh, we're going to the cabin Colorado rented."

He frowned and slowed the Jeep down to a crawl. Leave it to Tennie to think about the case. "No, there's nothing out here but the river."

"What are we going to do, go fishing?" The dirt road had turned into a path with barely enough room for the Jeep to get through.

"Do you want to go fishing?" He never pictured her as the fishing type, but then again he had envisioned Tennie only doing two things, one being detective work and the second was pure male fantasy. He wanted to get to know the real Tennessee Montgomery. If fishing made her happy and relaxed, he would turn around and head back into town. Surely there had to be someplace he could pick up a few poles and some bait.

She glanced curiously at Reece. "I don't like fishing. I think it's heartless to watch some poor little fish struggle against some monster-size hook in its mouth."

"Good."

"Good?"

"Yeah, good." Reece looked over at her and grinned. "I didn't bring any fishing poles."

"Then what are we doing out in the middle of nowhere?"

"Hiding." He turned the last bend and came to a clearing a good fifty feet above the river. The manager of the inn had been right, it was the perfect place. Peaceful, quiet, and as Tennie put it, miles from nowhere. He parked the Jeep away from the overlook.

"What are we hiding from?" Tennie looked around with interest. The Roaring River rushed by below them, dense woods surrounded them, and a crystal-blue sky was above them.

"Not what, but who." He opened his door and reached in the back of the Jeep.

Tennie smiled at the thick blanket and the wicker picnic basket he pulled out, but frowned at the pair of binoculars. "I give, who are we hiding from"—she glanced at the thick black binoculars—"and what are they for?"

"We're hiding from everyone, and these"—he held up the binoculars—"are for watching the animals." He looked at the river below. "See that spot right there?" He pointed to a small little nook. "The manager of the inn said that it's a favored watering hole."

Tennie shielded her eyes and studied the little cove. She didn't see any animals. "What kind of animals are we talking about?"

Reece spread the blanket on a bed of soft grass and away from any rocks. "I didn't ask." He placed the basket at one corner. "Is it important?"

She raised the binoculars and scanned the area. Nothing. "If we are talking about cute little bunnies, then no, it isn't important. But, if you're talking about grizzly bears, then yes, I think it's very important."

His brows came together in a deep frown. He took the binoculars from Tennie and checked out their surroundings. "There aren't any grizzlies in this area."

"Then how did the Grizzly's Revenge get its name?" She sat down on the blanket and raised her face toward the sun. It was turning out to be a gorgeous spring day. She unzipped her jacket and kept her face turned upward.

Reece was stumped. He had lived his entire life in San Francisco and considered cracked concrete, rough terrain. The closest he ever came to a wild and savage animal was the time he confronted the cheating husband of a very well-to-do lady. He looked at their Jeep and his frown deepened. With its top down it offered them absolutely no protection from any bloodthirsty savage grizzlies that happened along. Even with its top up a bear could shred the canvas like tissue paper. Great! All he wanted was to spend a quiet day alone with Tennie so they could concentrate on each other, not get her mauled to death. "Maybe we should look for another spot?"

"No way, José, this is perfect." She relaxed farther and allowed the warmth of the sun and the tranquil sound of the racing river to wash over her.

Tennie glanced at the silent man sitting stiffly beside her and sighed. What had happened to the sweet romantic man who had swept her away from her meddling family? Reece was clutching the binoculars. For the past hour he had been checking out the watering hole, the thick woods behind them, the thick woods on the other side of the river, and even the crystal-blue skies above them. A chipmunk hadn't a prayer in the world of approaching their picnic basket without being spotted.

She reached over, palmed a small rock, and hid it behind her back. She was tired of the nonexistent wildlife getting more attention than she. "So handsome, tell me again how many people were mauled to death by crazed grizzlies last year."

"That's not funny, Tennie." He lowered the binoculars for a moment and glared at her. "Are you ready to go?"

"We haven't eaten yet." She opened the basket and grinned.

"We can eat on the way back to the inn."

Tennie pulled out a bottle of white wine and two glasses. "This isn't the kind of lunch you can munch on while you drive, Reece." She lifted out apples, cheeses, grapes, and a loaf of French bread. "This is perfect."

"I guess it wouldn't hurt if we ate fast."

She swiped a piece of cheese, thinking of how Reece had unknowingly pushed all the right buttons. She wasn't leaving here until she made him put down those ugly binoculars and pay a little attention to her. She probably wouldn't see him for another year.

"You're ignoring this wonderful lunch"—she waved a hand over the meal—"as much as you've been neglecting me."

"I haven't been neglecting you!"

"No? What do you call it?"

"I've been protecting you."

"I don't need your protection," she said. "There aren't any furious beasts lurking nearby." She placed a couple of pieces of cheese and some grapes on a plate and handed it to him. "I could do with a lunch companion, though."

He took the plate. "What do we do if some hungry bear shows up during our meal?"

"We offer him some wine and a hunk of bread." She smiled as Reece pulled the binocular strap over his head and placed them into the basket.

Reece popped a grape into his mouth. "Have I ever told you how much I admire your spunk?"

"Spunk?" Tennie made a face and tore off a piece of bread. "My parents call it muleheadedness and my brother calls it stupidity. I don't think I'm any of those things when I'm around you."

"You're not?" he asked in surprise. "What are you then?"

"Confused"—she quickly glanced up once through her lowered lashes—"and scared."

"About what?"

"Me," she pushed a green grape out of her cheese pile and added, "us." She sighed deeply. "Every time I'm around you I get confused about my feelings. One minute I want to throttle you—that I can understand and live with."

"So what scares you about your feelings toward me?"

"It's the other times."

"What other times?"

"The times when I want to make love to you." She looked up and held his gaze. Honesty was a hell of a thing.

"How often does that occur?"

"Lately?"

"Yes." It was extremely difficult to answer when he had stopped breathing.

"About every time we are together." The first time she had met him the feeling had taken her by surprise; by the second reunion she had suppressed any desire she might have felt. This year was the worst. His sweet hot kisses had ignited a maelstrom of emotion she could no longer deny. She wanted Reece.

He sucked in his breath and nearly choked. "What scares you about making love with me?"

"That we aren't going to."

"We aren't?"

"No."

"Why aren't we?"

"Because I don't do one-night stands, no matter how tempting they appear."

"Who's talking about one night?"

"Correction, I don't do one-*reunion* stands."

"Who said anything about a one-*reunion* stand?"

"What else could it be, Reece? In case you forgot, you live on the West Coast while I live in the corn basket of America. It's not like we could go to the movies on Friday night and come Saturday morning pig out on pizza."

"First off I never eat pizza before noon," he said. "And whatever happened to compromise?"

"Great, how about if I meet you in Casper, Wyoming, for coffee and a quickie next Thursday?"

"That's not what I meant," snapped Reece. He shoved his fingers through his hair and glared at her.

"What exactly did you mean?"

"I don't know." He pushed away his plate. Tennie admitted to wanting him with one breath, and then proceeded to place obstacles in their path with her next. Women! Who could figure them out? "You better come up with a better excuse than that, though. Thousands of couples have beat the distance barriers in their relationships. We can if we *both* want to."

"We certainly aren't a couple, and the only relationship we have is the fact that your mother is now married to my uncle."

"Nix the family connection, Tennie." He leaned in closer and smiled. The barriers were becoming mighty thin. "We aren't related in the least."

"What about being opposites?"

"Didn't you ever hear about how they attract?" His smile turned into a wicked grin as he moved in closer.

Tennie leaned back and nearly ended up lying across the blanket with Reece bearing down on her. "You say that now, but I'm a hopeless slob. I eat every meal out, including breakfast, I have killer dust balls under my bed, and I don't even own an ironing board."

"Is all that supposed to make me stop wanting you?"

She blinked. "It doesn't?"

"Not by a long shot." He brushed her mouth with his.

"What about the fact that we're both detectives?"

"It means we have a better understanding about our careers and the toll they could take." His fingers grazed the wisps of fine golden hair gently blowing across her forehead.

"But we are so competitive." His mouth muffled her voice.

"That means we usually get what we want." He raised his head and gazed down into her confused hazel eyes. "I want you, Tennie."

"I know."

"You want me too."

"That's undeniable. But that doesn't mean it's the smartest thing to do."

"I'm not going to rush you, Tennie." He gently teased the corner of her mouth with his and coaxed a smile across her lips. "We take it real slow"—his teeth tenderly nipped at the fullness of her lower lip—"real slow."

Tennie melted under his heat and allowed him to set the pace.

Tennie leaned against her hotel room door and smiled. "Did I thank you for dinner yet?"

"Twice." Reece lightly kissed that captivatingly smiling mouth. "But I'm not complaining." They had spent the entire afternoon curled up on the blanket at the edge of the river, exchanging heated kisses and stories. When dusk started to fall they had decided to avoid the family and Little Lincoln and headed in the direction of Wellington. They had ended up eating dinner in a little out-of-the-way restaurant where it didn't matter what you were wearing and the food was excellent.

She sighed as his lips left hers. "It was a wonderful day, Reece. I really enjoyed myself."

"That was the idea." He took the key from her fingers and unlocked the door. He had noticed the hesitancy still in her eyes and knew tonight wasn't going to end the way he wanted it to. "Get a good night's sleep and I'll see you in the morning." He could wait a little longer for her to be sure. Today had been only the beginning.

"Can we go see Henrietta tomorrow?"

"First thing in the morning." He kissed her with hot need bordering on the edge of insanity. He broke the kiss before it slipped over the edge, and gently pushed her into her room before his control vanished.

"Sleep tight, Tennie." He pulled the door closed with a moan of frustration.

The Jeep came to a stop. Tennie's mouth fell open as two vicious geese charged her door and others nipped at the bumper. Loud hissing sounds and a series of noisy honks coming from the side of the house drew her attention. Five more geese came waddling across the yard and joined the others. Tennie looked at Reece and saw her horror echoed in his face. "Now what do we do, Sherlock?"

He shuddered as the savage group of geese continued their assault on the bumper. He unconsciously dropped one of his hands onto his lap. Memories of Ralph Stone's miserable expression the other day clouded his vision. The poor man had lost his manhood because of these nasty overgrown ovenstuffers. There was no way in hell he was getting out of the Jeep. "We could call Henrietta and Stan and see if they would meet us someplace."

Tennie eyed the distance between her door and the house. She knew she could outrun them, but visions of Alfred Hitchcock's *The Birds* kept her rooted to her seat. "Do you have their number?"

Before Reece could answer, a woman came out of the house toward them. She appeared to be somewhere in her sixties and amazingly agile as she shooed the geese away. "Get away from that Jeep, you bad, bad geese." She fluttered her apron at the hissing mass of feathers. "Now shoo, or there won't be any dessert tonight."

Tennie felt her mouth fall open as two of the smallest geese backed away. The woman smiled fondly at the two. "That's my good girls. Bo-Peep and Miss Muffett know how much Mommy loves them." She moved closer to the remaining boisterous critters and clapped her hands. "Humpty and Dumpty, get away from there." Two more geese backed away. "Jack and Jill, I won't be warning you two again." Tennie and Reece watched in utter amazement as two more left and made their way across the yard. The woman put her hands on her hips and stared at the lone goose still standing defiantly by the bumper. "Georgie Porgie, guess what we're having for dessert?" The goose cocked his head and seemed to be listening. The woman slowly smiled. "Cherry pie." In a flutter of feathers and some loud honking the goose waddled his way across the yard and around the side of the house.

The woman watched him go, then wiped her hands on her apron and smiled. "Hello. Sorry about that. They love bumpers or mirrors. Anything that shines."

Tennie got out and shook the woman's hand. "They also seem to love dessert." She cautiously glanced around the yard waiting for a second frontal attack. "Hello, you must be Henrietta Marino. I'm Tennie Montgomery and this is Reece Carpenter. We're investigating the murder of Tailpipe Taylor. Do you have a few minutes to spare?"

Henrietta nervously ran her hands down her flour-streaked apron and glanced anxiously around. "Now?"

"If you don't mind," Tennie said.

Reece got out of the Jeep and walked toward them without taking his gaze from the corner of the house. "We really would appreciate it."

"Well . . ." Henrietta glanced over her shoulder at the house behind her. "My husband's watching television right now."

"We need to ask him some questions too." Tennie expertly maneuvered Henrietta into walking toward the house.

"Stan gets upset if you interrupt him during his favorite show."

"How about if we ask you some questions first. Then when his show is finished, we can talk to him."

Reece held open the screen door as the ladies entered the kitchen. "What's his favorite show?" he asked politely.

"*Reel, Rods, and Rivers.* Please keep your voices down." She waved a hand toward the kitchen chairs. "You might as well have a seat."

Tennie and Reece shared a glance before they sat. Tennie lowered her voice and asked, "You mean your husband sits in the living room and watches other men fish." It sounded as exciting as sitting in front of a television and watching corn grow.

"Twice a day. Once in the morning and once in the afternoon." She went over to the counter where two pies stood ready to be baked. Two cherry pies.

"How well did you know Tailpipe?" Tennie asked.

Henrietta opened the oven door and placed the pies inside. "Not too well. I know his wife Emma Sue a lot better." She kept her back to them. With trembling hands she set the timer. "We saw each other at church every Sunday."

"Was Emma Sue the kind of woman to have an affair?"

"Oh my, no," Henrietta cried.

"You don't think she was seeing my uncle Colorado?"

"No, I don't." Henrietta started briskly to wipe down the already immaculate countertop. "Neither does anyone else in our church."

"What about Tailpipe?"

The dishcloth stopped in midwipe. Henrietta kept her gaze on the counter and absently rubbed at one spot. "What about him?"

"Did you know he was having an affair with your sister-in-law, Pricilla?"

"Everyone in Little Lincoln knew that. It was the talk of the town for years."

"*Was* the talk of the town?" Tennie questioned. "You mean it hasn't been recently?"

"After six years even Little Lincoln would consider it old news." She moved on to another imaginary spot of dirt on the counter.

"How did Emma Sue handle the knowledge that her husband was having an affair?"

"In the beginning she put up a brave front." She

anxiously straightened the quilted cover over the toaster. "Over the years I think she accepted it and even was somewhat relieved."

"Relieved?"

"From what I heard, Tailpipe was a very active man." A blush swept her cheeks. "Emma Sue and him weren't in love any longer. They haven't been for years. They just kind of lived together to fight off the loneliness." Henrietta glanced at Tennie. "They never had any children, only each other."

"I see." Tennie silently glanced at Reece and mustered up a sad little smile. The whole thing sounded depressing to her. "Henrietta, I would like to ask you one more question if I may?"

Henrietta nodded and twisted her hands beneath her apron.

"Do you have any idea who might want to kill Tailpipe?"

Tears flooded the woman's eyes. "No one wanted to kill Tailpipe. He was a good man in his own way." The tears welled up and overflowed down her cheek. "It must have been some type of accident."

Tennie frowned at the desperation in her voice. "Your husband went to the police and said he saw my uncle outside Tailpipe's garage the morning he was murdered."

"So?" Both Tennie and Reece quickly turned to the large man standing in the doorway to the living room. Neither one of them had heard him coming.

Reece stood up and held out his hand. "Mr. Marino, I presume?"

Stan glanced at the offered hand and then at his wife, who had turned deadly pale. "You been gossiping again?"

Tennie quickly stood up and flashed her most charming smile. "Hello, Mr. Marino. May I call you Stan?" Not waiting for a reply she went on, "I'm Tennie Montgomery and this is my partner, Reece Carpenter. We're investigating the death of Tailpipe Taylor."

Stan glared down at Tennie and didn't return her smile. "So?"

Tennie mentally pulled herself together. "I understand that you were the one who saw my uncle near Tailpipe's garage the morning of his death."

"So?"

She gritted her teeth and refused to glance at Reece. "You happened to be in the area?"

"I was driving down the street, minding my own business."

"And you saw Colorado?" Reece asked.

"Yeah." Stan marched over to the kitchen door and opened it. It was a silent command to leave.

Tennie and Reece moved closer to the door. Tennie glanced at Henrietta in sympathy. The poor woman looked ready to collapse. "One more question, Mr. Marino." She looked up and locked gazes with the older man. Somewhere in his past life, Stan Marino had to have been Paul Bunyan. "Why did you go to the police and report my uncle?"

Stan's mere size forced Tennie and Reece from the house. Before he closed the door he answered Tennie's question. "Because I'm a concerned citizen." His evil sneer as the door slammed belied his answer.

Reece grabbed Tennie's arm and hurried her to the Jeep. He didn't want the geese to see them and decide the hell with the cherry pie. He slammed her Jeep door and hurried around to the driver's side. Without wasting a moment he pulled away from the curb. He glanced at Tennie's puzzled face. "Well, that was interesting."

Tennie stared back over her shoulder at the house fading in the distance. "It was sad, Reece, not interesting. She named the geese, did you see that?"

"She also bakes pies for them, Tennie. The woman is gone."

She had to agree with Reece on that call. Henrietta acted like a regular on a David Lynch television series. "I think she was hiding something."

"Probably a skeleton in the closet." He turned toward the center of town. "A real skeleton."

Tennie rezipped her coat. "I don't like Stan. He's uglier than a junkyard dog, and twice as mean."

Reece kept driving. "Want to visit Colorado?"

"Sure, maybe we'll get lucky."

"Tennie?"

She slipped on her sunglasses. She didn't want

Colorado to see the signs of her sleepless night and worry. "Yes?"

"Would you like to go out to dinner tonight?" Reece felt the rush of excitement pulse through his body. He was going to have Tennie all to himself again.

"You mean at the lodge tonight?"

"No, I mean you and me and about twenty miles of highway between the family and us." He tenderly brushed her rosy cheeks and frowned at the sunglasses. More accurately he frowned at the signs of a sleepless night she was trying to hide. "We'll have dinner and go dancing." His finger lingered on her lower lip. Was he the cause of her sleepless night? "We won't discuss the case at all."

"It sounds like heaven, Reece." Regretfully, she added, "But I can't."

"Why not?"

"Because I promised Montana and Sue Ellen that I would baby-sit so they could have a night out on the town."

"You're going to watch all four boys?" If the idea didn't strike him as so funny, he might have been crushed by her rejection.

"Don't you dare laugh, Reece."

"I can't help it." He burst out laughing. "I keep thinking about last year when they left you in charge for an afternoon, and then there were only the three."

Tennie yanked her arm away. "It wasn't my fault

that alarm went off and half the hotel had to be evacuated." She shuddered at the distant memories. "Besides, North and South Carolina will be helping me tonight. I figure with the three of us, we should be able to control the monsters."

Reece had his doubts. He had seen how much Tennie loved her nephews. So much, that she allowed them to get away with murder. Which reminded him. . . . He got out of the Jeep and joined Tennie on the sidewalk. They walked toward the alley. "I noticed one particularly interesting piece of information today."

"What's that?"

"Do you know that television show Stan was watching?"

"Reel, Rods, and Rivers? His all-time favorite. The one he never misses an episode of."

"Yes, that's the one."

"So what's so interesting about that?" Tennie stopped in front of the police department's door.

"Didn't you notice that it's on at exactly the same time as when Tailpipe was murdered. Wasn't Stan supposed to be driving down the street minding his own business when he spotted Colorado near Tailpipe's garage?" He grinned at Tennie's reaction. She hadn't picked up on that clue. He ushered her into the station. "Amazing how he missed the episode on that particular morning, isn't it?"

EIGHT

Tennie barely heard the pounding on the hotel room door above Galveston's wailing. She shifted the small bundle in her arms and hurried to the door. "It's about time you got here—" She blinked in confusion at Reece standing in the middle of the hall. "What are you doing here? Where's North and South Carolina?"

"They aren't coming." Reece smiled at the picture she made standing there with a baby in her arms. If you ignored the wild-eyed look and the slight trembling of her lower lip, she was the picture of a radiant and loving new mother.

She looked frantically up and down the hall trying to unravel some sick joke. "What do you mean, they aren't coming?" Two-year-old Houston streaked out from behind her and headed down the hall.

Reece reached out and caught the boy by his shoulder. He smiled. Houston was wearing a 49er's sweatshirt, one navy blue sock, and nothing else. He bit his lip to keep the laughter from spilling out. "I ran into them downstairs. They both had a date with Altman and seemed concerned that you might not be able to handle the boys alone."

She glared at the laughter lurking in his eyes. "Great! Now what am I supposed to do?" Galveston let out another ear-piercing wail.

"Don't worry. I volunteered to help out." He turned Houston around and gently propelled him back into the room. "What's Galveston's problem and why is Houston streaking in the halls?"

Tennie closed the door behind him and leaned against it. He wasn't the Carolina twins, but he was an extra pair of hands. She couldn't afford to scare him off. "I have no idea what's wrong with Galveston, and Houston just visited the potty." She tried to smile confidently.

Austin and Dallas came tumbling through the open door from the connecting bedroom. "Uncle Reece!" shouted Austin.

Tennie watched and frowned as Reece bent down and pulled the boys apart. She had seen Montana do that a thousand times, but each time she tried the same move she always ended up in the middle of the free-for-all. What was it, some kind of male thing? "Boys, I thought I told you to get ready for dinner?"

Austin and Dallas looked at each other and shrugged their shoulders. "We are ready, Aunt Tennie."

She lightly bounced the crying Galveston and

glared at the boys. "I think not. March yourselves right back in there and put on something that doesn't have any holes in it." Both boys wore jeans with holes in the knees; four-year-old Dallas's shirt was turned inside out.

Austin muttered something about girls under his breath as they turned around and went back into their room. Tennie moved Galveston to her shoulder and lightly patted his back as she glanced down at Houston. If he wasn't so adorable, she'd give him a lecture on morals. "What am I to do with you, young man?"

Houston grinned, climbed up onto the bed, and started to bounce. "Lost me undies."

Tennie prayed that he hadn't flushed them down the toilet. Austin had pulled that number on her four years before at the family reunion in Chicago. Montana wasn't really impressed when Sue Ellen and he came back from a night out and found housekeeping mopping up their flooded hotel room. "Where did you take them off, Houston?"

Houston bounced once more and rolled onto the floor. "Potty room." Tennie groaned as he headed toward the bathroom calling "Scooby-doo, where are you?"

Reece watched the natural way she held Galveston and patted his tiny back. Tennie had more maternal instincts than she had given herself credit for. "Why's Houston calling 'Scooby-doo' if he lost his underwear?"

"Me found! Me found!" Houston came running out of the bathroom, waving a pair of underwear like a flag.

Reece chuckled as he saw the underwear. Scooby-doo was printed all over them. "I hope he doesn't wear the same kind of underwear his whole entire life," Reece murmured.

Tennie grinned. "At least it won't be boring." She jerked in surprise as Galveston let out a loud burp. "Well, young man, was that your problem?" He closed his eyes and nestled snugly against her.

Reece laughed. For such a little one, Galveston sure packed a wallop. "Are you taking the kids down to the dining room for dinner?"

"That was the plan." She glanced at Austin and Dallas as they came back into the room and at Houston who had managed to put his underwear on by himself, even if it was on backward. "Maybe I should call room service?" She didn't know what would be worse, food fights in the hotel room, or being scrutinized by her relatives who seemed to enjoy standing back and watching catastrophe after catastrophe happen whenever she baby-sat Montana's tribe. Last year there was even a pool on how long she would hold out before calling her mother for help. Tennie had bet twenty bucks she would last the entire time. She had won a grand total of sixty bucks and a headache that lasted for days.

"Don't call room service. I'm sure between the two of us we can manage to keep them under control." He looked at the three boys standing by the bed. "If you guys behave yourselves and eat your dinner, I'll let you order anything you want from the dessert menu."

Smiles flashed brighter than flashbulbs. "Really! Neat-o."

Tennie laughed. Maybe it wouldn't be so bad with Reece there. "If you help Houston finish dressing, I'll change Galveston and see if I can figure out how to put him in that seat Sue Ellen is always carrying him in."

In a few minutes she glanced up and saw Reece and all three boys quietly standing by the door. She was impressed. It would have taken her at least another thirty minutes before she had them all ready. She carefully placed Galveston in his carrier and fastened the safety harness. She placed the strap of a diaper bag over her shoulder and picked up the carrier. "Ready." She joined the parade of males as they walked out the door and down the hall.

A smile tugged at her lips as Reece took the blue-striped diaper bag from her and carried it into the dining room full of relatives. For some strange reason the floppy-eared dog embroidered onto the side of the bag suited him. The three boys behind him tried to keep up with his steps. Austin did an admirable job, Dallas was a tad behind, and Houston's little legs were moving as fast as they could. Reece Carpenter was born to be a father. She glanced down at the infant she was carrying. Well, maybe . . .

Galveston's huge blue eyes stared back at her. She smiled and the baby let out a wail that shook the china.

Every head in the dining room turned and looked at her. Tennie raised her chin and walked to the table where Reece stood waiting. She had read the message flashing in her relatives' eyes as clearly as if it had been broadcast over an intercom: *Gentlemen, place your bets.*

Reece heard the key in the door and stood up to stretch. Montana and Sue Ellen had returned. He smiled as they came through the door and put his finger to his lips. Tennie was sound asleep in a chair with her feet propped up on the bed. Galveston was cuddled up on her chest, snoring away. About an hour before when Reece realized they were both out, he had covered them and turned off the television. He had spent the last hour watching Tennie sleep and thinking.

He was in love with Tennie. He always thought that when he fell in love it would be simultaneous. He would look across some crowded room and spot the woman of his dreams. She would turn her head, see him, and fall in love. It hadn't happened that way. Somewhere over the last two years Tennie had bullied her way into his heart and wouldn't vacate those premises. He moved over to Tennie and the sleeping infant and gently removed the blanket. She shifted slightly and moaned. Galveston sighed.

Reece smiled as her eyes slowly opened and blinked up at him. He wondered what she would do when he declared his love to her and to the rest of the family. Because he wasn't wasting another year until the next reunion, or attending every family function hoping to catch a glimpse of her. "Shhh, sleepyhead. They're back." He moved aside and let Sue Ellen remove Galveston from her chest.

Tennie stretched. Montana was looking around the room in utter amazement. He quietly pushed open the interconnecting door and checked on the three sleeping boys in the next room. He came back scratching his head. "Okay, what happened?"

"Nothing happened," Tennie snapped. She kept her voice down so she wouldn't wake Galveston, whom Sue Ellen was placing in his crib.

"Come on, Tennie, this is big brother you're talking to. I was fairly astonished when we returned and there weren't any fire trucks outside the hotel. When we crossed the lobby and didn't see any harried-looking employees, I began to worry. Now I come back from a terrific night out with my lady and I find all four of my sons in their pajamas and sound asleep. I demand to know what happened."

Tennie ignored Reece's and Sue Ellen's chuckles as she stepped toe-to-toe with Montana. "Absolutely nothing happened. There were no fires, floods, or food fights. Reece and I took the kids to dinner, then we played some video games in the recreation room downstairs. The boys took a bath, got into their pajamas, and watched television for an hour before they went to bed. The only problem we had is

Galveston doesn't like to be put down. So I held him for the entire time."

"You didn't call Mom at all tonight?" Montana asked.

Understanding started to dawn. "How much did you bet?" Her own brother had set her up.

"I didn't bet any money, Tennie. What kind of brother do you think I am?"

"You don't want me to answer that right now." She crossed her arms and squinted. "Just what did you bet that I wouldn't last the evening?"

"I bet Sue Ellen a week's worth of night feedings." He glanced at his son sleeping in the rental crib and sighed.

"It should have been a month." Tennie looked at Sue Ellen. "Thank you for having enough faith in me when my own brother didn't."

Sue Ellen smiled and linked her arm through Montana's. "It's not that he doesn't have faith in you, Tennie. Do you really think he would allow you to watch the boys if he questioned your ability?"

"That's what it's beginning to look like to me." Tennie couldn't hide the hurt that had entered her voice. She grabbed her oversize purse and headed for the door.

Reece frowned and Sue Ellen shoved Montana forward. "Tennie, wait," said Montana. "I didn't mean to hurt you. Sue Ellen's right, I would never allow you to watch the boys if I didn't believe you could handle them. They are my life, Tennie. When I left here tonight, I knew I could trust you to keep them safe." He stepped forward and tapped her on the tip of her nose. "Do you know how I knew that?"

"How?"

"Because you love them as much as I do."

He opened his arms and Tennie hugged him. It was one of the nicest things he had ever said to her. "Thanks." She moaned as he squeezed harder and laughed.

"Since you did such a fantastic job tonight, how would you like to watch them tomorrow night?"

Tennie stared in horror at Montana. He couldn't possibly be serious. Reece pushed her toward the door and opened it. "Sorry, Montana, but my partner and I have plans for tomorrow night," he said, pushing her out into the hall.

"Well how about—"

"No can do, Montana. This case is a tricky one." He closed the door as Montana and Sue Ellen started to laugh. He noticed Tennie's thoughtful expression as he walked her through the halls to their rooms. "Penny for your thoughts."

Tennie came out of her daze and glanced around. They were standing outside her door. "Oh, sorry, Reece." She started to dig through her tote, looking for the key. "My thoughts aren't worth that."

He leaned against the door and smiled as she dug deeper. By the look of things it was going to take a metal detector to find the key. "Did you ever think of carrying a smaller purse?"

She handed him her checkbook, two paperbacks, a pack of cookies, a can of Cheez Whiz, and a brand-new toothbrush still in its wrapper. She opened the tote wider and practically climbed inside it. "What for?"

Reece wasn't positive, but he would have sworn her voice echoed. "You might be able to find your keys easier."

Tennie swore as something poked her finger. "Damn." In a triumphal wave she pulled the lone key from the depths of the purse. "I can find my keys now." She started to repack the tote. "If I had a smaller purse what would I do with all my stuff?"

Reece glanced at the paperback Spanish/English dictionary in his hand and chuckled. "How many times have you had to use Spanish while on a case?"

"Only once." She carefully took the book from him, gave it a loving pat, and dropped it into the bag. "And that once taught me never to go anywhere without this dictionary."

Reece was about to ask her what she meant but decided against it. It might be better if he didn't know. Being in love was a strain on any man, being in love with Tennie could prove to be fatal. He took the key from her fingers and inserted it into the lock.

"Have I thanked you for all your help tonight?"

"No." He gently pulled her closer and brushed his lips across her mouth. Love and tenderness sparkled in his eyes. "Thank me now."

She was momentarily thrown off balance by the

look that had leapt into his gaze. What was he feeling? Was he experiencing the same kind of excitement she was feeling whenever they were close? Did his heart pound and his fingers tremble? Did he feel the heat? Her gaze caressed his face for an answer. Desire, passion, and need were clearly there, but what was that elusive light glowing in his eyes? She rose up onto her toes and softly pressed her lips against his.

Reece groaned and deepened the kiss. This was the woman he loved. He plunged his tongue into her mouth and savored her sweetness. Her heat. This was the woman he wanted to spend the rest of his life getting to know. He lightly nipped at her lower lip.

Tennie broke the kiss and came up gasping for air. She could drown in Reece's hot kisses and never complain. "Are you coming in tonight?" It was a blatant invitation, and they both knew it.

Reece studied the post-and-beam ceiling of the hallway. He would have given anything to say yes. Anything except the chance to win her love. He needed to slow down. He needed to give her time to know what she was getting into. He was playing for keeps. His voice crackled with tension. "Not tonight, Tennie." He pushed open her door and gently eased her into the room. If he stepped over the threshold it would be his undoing. He was only human after all. "I'll see you at breakfast." The door softly closed behind her. He leaned his forehead against the wall as his fingers turned white gripping the rough wood molding. Control was slow in coming.

Tennie blinked in confusion at the inside of her door. The fire evacuation chart blurred before her eyes. What had gone wrong this time? The soft sound of Reece closing his hotel room door filtered through to her. A moment later the sound of his shower being turned on full force caused her to say a very unladylike word. In a frustrated rage she picked up her coat and stormed out of the room. With any luck the Sierras would get their last snowstorm of the season tonight. A fierce blinding blizzard sounded perfect right about now.

Five minutes later Tennie sat on the secluded bench beneath two huge pine trees and thought. It was only eleven o'clock at night, but she hadn't seen another living soul since she left the lodge's lobby and headed for the bench which she had found the other night when she had stormed out of the lodge in frustration. Tonight it felt familiar and inviting. It was the perfect spot for thinking.

Reece! How could one man be so infuriating and yet so lovable? How could he get her hotter than the back room of Freddie the Fence's pawnshop with just one look? How could he inspire lust, sinful desires, and homicidal thoughts all within the space of five minutes? How could he keep walking away from the best thing she ever had felt?

Tennie pulled her legs up and wrapped her arms around her knees. The night was chilly and clear, and the freshness of the air seemed to burn her lungs with its purity. Not a blizzard in sight. The stars were so close, she felt as if she could reach out and touch them. It was the perfect night for falling in love. She glared at the lodge and found Reece's room. His light was still on. Good, with any luck he would have a sleepless night too.

Someone was playing a horrible joke on her, or Cupid's arrows had missed their mark by a mile. There was no way she should have fallen in love with Reece, but she had. Chemistry she could have understood. Physical desires, lust, call it what you would, she could have dealt with all those feelings, but love scared the starch out of her. What was she supposed to do now? Pack Reece up and take him back home to Hogs Hollow, Iowa, with her?

She frowned at his window as the light went off. Great! He was climbing into his big bed with visions of sugar plums dancing in his head and she was sitting outside freezing her tush off with her sexual engine at full throttle.

Tennie rested her cheek on her shivering knees and continued to stare at the darkened window. She wanted Reece. Reece wanted her. The only thing stopping them from exploring the endless possibilities that entailed was Reece. He had some twisted logic that she needed to be sure first. Sure of what? That she loved him? That she desired him? That she wouldn't regret sharing his bed, body, and a few hot showers with him?

She already knew the answers and she was sure. Sure that she would regret not sharing her love with Reece, if only for the week. Happily-ever-after wasn't included in this family reunion. But for now, she'd take what she could get. Who did Reece think he was calling all the shots? For the last two years he had marched into the Montgomerys' reunion and had gotten his way. Well not this year! This was her year to prove exactly what a Montgomery was made of.

Blood rushed toward her frozen toes as she stood up and walked purposefully toward the lodge's entrance. Reece Carpenter had better beware; she was running on all eight cylinders and heading for the checkered flag.

Reece heard the interconnecting door open and stopped breathing. For the past fifteen minutes he had been staring at the ceiling, wondering what Tennie would do if he opened that door and joined her in her bed. He glanced at the opening and frowned. So much for sexual fantasies. He couldn't read the expression on her face because the light was coming from behind her, but he could see she was dressed to go out. Something must be wrong. "Where are you going?"

"Here." Her voice was a whisper in the dark. She slowly unzipped the coat.

He sat up in bed taking the blanket with him. He didn't want her to see what her sudden appearance in his room had done to his anatomy. "Why are you wearing your coat?"

Tennie shrugged and the coat landed with a soft thud at her feet. "I'm not."

He watched in astonishment as she kicked off her sneakers and sent them sailing toward a chair. Surely she wasn't doing what he thought she was doing. He cleared his throat and asked, "Are you returning the socks you borrowed?"

She tugged off the socks and smiled as they hit the floor somewhere near the discarded coat. "Nope." With the gentle light spilling in from her room she could see every emotion crossing his face. She smiled at his bewilderment. A taste of his own medicine wouldn't kill him. Her heart and body pounded at the desire revealed there. His jaw was clenched and his mouth was set in a grim line.

The love she felt overflowed her heart and swam through her senses as hope leapt into his gaze. Her trembling fingers grabbed hold of the hem of her oversize sweater and pulled the garment slowly over her head.

Reece sucked in his breath and nearly choked on his desire. "Tennie?" She was standing by the foot of his bed and in the semidarkness he could make out the generous proportions of her breasts being contained by a lacy dark bra. He moved to get out of bed.

"No, don't." She toyed with the snap on her jeans. Tennie knew she wasn't the most beautiful woman in the world, but the way Reece was staring gave her the impression that she was. She liked having Reece lying in bed watching her undress. If he touched her now, she would go off faster than a fifty-cent firecracker and never have this memory. The snap coming undone sounded like a shot being fired.

He was scared to move for fear he would wake up and realize this was all a dream. He felt each tooth of the metal zipper clicking its way through the tab of her jeans. "Tennie, do you know what you are doing?" God, he hoped so!

She placed both her hands on her hips and slightly tilted her head. Her golden ponytail swished over one pale shoulder and barely covered one of her breasts. "Am I doing something wrong?"

He couldn't take his eyes off the gap left by the unzipped jeans. "No!" Her pale smooth skin was showing through, enticing him beyond endurance. "Unless this is a dream."

"This most definitely is not a dream, Reece." Her fingers slowly inched the jeans down her legs. She had never stripped for a man before, then again she'd never been in love before either. She was half nerves and half elation. With two graceful steps she was closer to the bed, leaving the denim behind.

Reece felt the blanket tent over his lap. So much for camouflage. It would take a quilt made of ice packs to keep his desire from showing. The dark silky panties that matched the bra were low in the front and cut high on the sides. "Vive la France."

Tennie smiled as her nervousness disappeared. "I

only have one thing to say to you, Reece, before I join you in that big old bed."

He could think of one very important thing he would love for her to say. He held his breath and waited impatiently. "That is?"

She squashed her natural impulse to shout her love and said the second thing that had popped into her mind. She grabbed the rubber band holding her ponytail and yanked it out of her hair. With a gentle shake of her head she sent silky golden hair flying in every direction. "Gentleman, start your engines."

NINE

Reece had no idea why she was talking like Richard Petty, but if it kept her where she was she could talk like Fred Flintstone for all he cared. He reached out for her and pulled her into his arms. "Tennie," he murmured against the smoothness of her neck, "please tell me you're sure."

She arched her neck farther back and clung to the hard warmth of his body. He was gloriously naked. "I'm sure of everything I need to be sure about."

"Thank God." His teeth gently nipped at the delicate lobe of her ear. "I don't think I'd have the strength to stop."

Her leg caressed the hard muscular contours of his outer thigh. It had been a very long time since she had been with a man, but there wasn't any awkwardness with Reece. She laughed softly. "Ahhh, but do you have the strength to go on?"

He growled playfully and pushed her onto her back. Golden hair was spread across his pillow. He couldn't remember being so relaxed with another woman. He nudged her hip with his manhood and saw the heated desire leap into her eyes. "Next question."

"Please tell me you're as organized and predictable as I have always given you credit for." Muscles rippled under her fingertips as she stroked his back, tracing every curve and valley.

His fingers tenderly brushed her cheeks and teased the corner of her smile with quick faint strokes. "Meaning?"

"You have some foiled little packets tucked away in the nightstand just in case this situation"—she nudged his manhood with her hips and grinned—"popped up."

"And if I don't?" He didn't mind being organized, it was the predictable that unnerved him. Damn, if she wasn't right again.

"Then I'm afraid I'm going to have to march my butt back into my room and start digging through my purse again. Somewhere in there I know I have a couple of cute condoms."

"Cute condoms!" Reece grinned at the notion. What the hell constituted a cute condom, pink bows printed on them?

"Yes, cute." She slid her fingers down to his tight buns and gave a light pinch. "I solved a case for the garden club back in Hogs Hollow. They happen to be a very concerned group of ladies and gentlemen, very 1990s." She licked the strong column of his neck. It tasted tangy and masculine, pure Reece. "Anyway, one of the dear souls discreetly passed me a couple of pink-foiled condoms for a job well done."

"Pink-foiled?" His knees went weak as Tennie traced his collarbone with her tongue.

"They're called Lady's Choice."

"Am I this lady's choice?"

"Most definitely." She trailed a string of kisses up his jaw and noticed that he had shaved recently. "Should I go get them?"

"No need." He caressed the satiny smoothness of her waist. "It seems I once again proved to be predictable." If it hadn't been for the fact it would have taken her half the night to find a lone pink-foiled packet in that storage bin of a purse, he wouldn't have told her about the precautions he had picked up in town the other night. He reached over to the nightstand and plucked a silver packet off its top.

"Reece, there's nothing wrong with being predictable." She teased the frown pulling at the corner of his mouth with the tip of her tongue. "I happen to find it very sexy."

He allowed her to continue to smooth away his frown. "You do?" His fingers unclasped the back catch on her bra and he slowly peeled the straps down her arms. He groaned as pale rounded breasts topped with dusky pert nipples brushed the curls covering his chest. The lacy forest-green bra landed somewhere over the side of the bed.

She captured his lower lip between her teeth and gently nipped. Her tongue quickly followed and laved the small imprints her teeth had left behind. She felt the shudder that racked his body and rejoiced in the knowledge that she had as much power over him as he was exhibiting over her. They were on equal footing.

Tennie trembled with desire as Reece lowered his head. His strong hands molded her breasts into high mountains, each with a darkened nub peeking out from between his fingers. The intensity gleaming in his dark gaze nearly sent her over the top. She had never felt such passion, need, and want in her life. The amazing part was, Reece had barely touched her. What was it going to feel like when he actually took her?

Reece brushed his thumbs over her nipples and smiled as they quivered. His warm breath softly caressed them. "For the past two years I have been dreaming about what color nipples you'd have." His tongue slowly circled one, causing a moan to escape Tennie. The faint light pouring in from her room was being blocked by his body but there was no way he was moving. His manhood was cradled between the heat of her thighs with only a sliver of silk separating him from heaven. The only thing that could persuade him to move was the need to do away with that silken barrier.

"Two years?" Had she heard him right?

He thrust his hips forward. "Two long and frustrating years, Tennie." He started to rock. "You drove me crazy during that first reunion." His tongue circled the other nipple with the same intense slowness. "Last year I was a complete basket case by the time the mystery was solved. I took so many cold showers last year, I was afraid the hotel would charge me extra for the number of towels I went through."

Her fingers softly kneaded the tight muscles clenched in his buttocks. "Why didn't you say something?"

Reece glanced up. He had expected her to laugh about it, not sound so disappointed. For the last two years they were going at each other's throats. Could she have possibly been feeling something besides aversion for him back then? "What would you have done?"

"Probably the same thing I've done now."

He picked up on the strange answer. Shouldn't she have said, doing now? "What have you done?"

Tennie held his gaze and swallowed hard. It was now or never. She was a Montgomery, and a Montgomery never ran or avoided a problem. Taking a deep breath she prayed she was crashing right into heaven. "I fell in love with you, Reece."

Reece felt the air leave his lungs. Love! Had she really said love? He read every emotion gleaming in the depths of her eyes and grinned. Love was shining the brightest. It overpowered the desire and need there. Tennie really did love him. He tenderly toyed with a wayward curl against her cheek. "That's a load off my mind."

"It is?"

"Hmmm. . . ." He brushed the ends of the curl over her cheek and across her kiss-moistened lips.

She wiggled her nose and pushed the curl away. "Why is it a load off your mind?" She didn't expect him to declare his undying love or anything, but a general recap of his feelings wouldn't go unnoticed.

He teased the curl down her throat and over the generous mounds of her breasts. "Because."

Tennie gritted her teeth and hissed, "Reece!" She didn't know what upset her more, the intense desire he made her feel or his being so obstinate.

"The reason I am so damn happy, Tennie, is that I've been racking my brains, trying to figure out how to make you fall in love with me."

Her fingers slid over his hips and threaded their way into the thick bush of curls surrounding his arousal. Two could play at his game. "Why did you want me to fall in love with you?"

Reece arched his back and stiffened. Her delicate little hot fingers were centimeters away from making him lose his iron-willed control. "Don't do that, Tennie. I can't think straight when you do that."

"Good," she smiled. Her fingers slowly moved a fraction closer.

"There's only one reason why I wanted you to fall in love with me, Tennie." He gnashed his teeth and sucked in some much needed air.

Her fingernail outlined the base of his throbbing manhood. "And that is?" she purred.

His control shattered. "Since I fell in love with you

two years ago, I wanted to make damn sure you loved me back." He arched into her hand and closed his eyes in ecstasy.

Tennie lightly stroked his silken length and grinned. He loved her back! "Ah, Reece." She reached up and kissed him, "You're such a romantic."

Tennie moved her foot and buried her head farther under the pillow. Something was tickling her toes. She heard a deep chuckle and peeked out from under the pillow. Someone was at the foot of the bed with his head under the blankets kissing her toes. "Reece?"

A soft kiss landed on her instep. "Who else were you expecting?"

"I wasn't expecting anyone"—she glanced at the window; dawn had barely broken—"at this ungodly hour." She wiggled her foot as his tongue traced her anklebone. "Do you have a foot fetish that I should know about?"

"Not until I met you." His lips brushed across the delicate instep of her other foot. Somehow in the heated passion of last night he had totally overlooked her feet. He had awakened to the first rays of morning with the ardent desire to taste every inch of Tennie. Starting with her gorgeous little toes.

She pulled the pillow back over her head. The man was crazy. The man was insatiable. She smiled. Well, not totally insatiable. There had been two times she could distinctly remember him laying there gasping for air and praying his heart wouldn't give out. Reece Carpenter had taken her twice to heaven during the night. Once the ride was so fast and frantic, it made Disneyland seem like a penny carnival, and once so slow and sweet, it had brought tears to her eyes. So this was love!

He nuzzled the sensitive skin on the back of her knee. "You just lie there, love. I'll do all the work."

She pretended she was asleep and tried to ignore the way her blood was heating up. Her fist clutched at the sheet as his mouth caressed the back of her thighs. He stroked her outer thighs with his fingers as he placed hot kisses up them.

Tennie's body dissolved into a puddle of need beneath his gifted mouth.

Half an hour later Tennie cuddled deeper into his embrace. Her breathing was almost back to normal and the soft downy curls covering his chest cushioned her cheek. She sighed in contentment and closed her eyes against the glare of the morning sun filtering through the windows.

Reece stroked the curtain of golden hair overflowing his chest. Lord, how he loved this woman.

Tennie mumbled sleepily, "I really ought to start taking vitamins."

He continued to hold her long after she fell asleep and the sun topped the distant mountains.

❖━━━━━━━━━❖

Tennie awoke for the second time to the distant murmuring of voices and the mouth-watering aroma of coffee. Somewhere in the lodge was a coffeepot with her name on it. She slowly opened her eyes and looked at the darkened windows. Reece must have pulled the curtains closed against the sun. She glanced at the empty spot beside her and then at the clock on the nightstand and groaned. It was after ten.

She jerked in surprise and yanked the sheets up to her chin as the interconnecting door to the rooms was pushed open. She relaxed her grip on the blankets when she saw it was only Reece with a room service cart.

"Ah, good. You're awake."

"Barely." Tennie pushed her hair out of her eyes and studied Reece. He was dressed in a pair of jeans and an old sweatshirt. He was barefoot, unshaven, and had a slightly wrinkled look as if he had dressed in a hurry. She had never seen him more relaxed or gorgeous. The man was turning her bones to jelly and she hadn't even had her morning coffee yet. She eyed the cart and the pot sitting there. "Please tell me that's coffee."

Reece moved the cart closer to the small table by the window. With sure hands he set the table, complete with a small crystal vase containing one lone pink carnation. "If you give me a morning kiss, I'll even pour it for you." Reece pulled the curtains open and light flooded the room.

Tennie wet her lips, unsure if she was anticipating the kiss or the coffee more. She glanced around the floor and noticed all her clothes from last night had been picked up and put away. "You wouldn't happen to have a robe, would you?" Last night in the fog of desire she hadn't worried too much about what Reece thought about her body, but under the dazzling morning sun streaking through the window, every imperfection would show with glaring clarity.

Reece smiled and leaned against the empty cart. Tennie looked ravishing, mussed, and entirely too lonely in that big bed. It took all his willpower to keep from rejoining her. "There isn't an inch of your gorgeous body I haven't seen"—his smile grew as her cheeks became flushed—"or tasted."

"I could say the same about you." She let her gaze travel down the length of his body. "But I notice you happen to be wearing clothes."

Desire tightened his body. Damn if she couldn't seduce him with a mere glance. He walked over to the bathroom and pulled a thick navy-blue robe off the back of the door. With a gentle smile he stood next to the bed and held the robe open for her.

She lifted her chin and released the sheets. With all the grace of a goddess she stood up and placed a light kiss on his mouth. "That's for my coffee." Before she lost her nerve she stepped into the robe and slowly tied the sash. She heard Reece groan before he turned away to stalk over to the table. She hid her triumphant smile behind a veil of tangled golden curls.

Reece pulled the Jeep to a stop in front of the office of the After Six Motel. So this was Tailpipe's notorious stomping grounds? It looked run down, badly in need of a paint job. Poor Pricilla sinking so low and Ralph quietly sitting by and allowing it to happen.

Tennie eyed the motel with disgust. Norman Bates would have felt right at home running the place. She got out of the Jeep and picked up her purse from the floor. She didn't like the way Reece was glaring at the office door. "Do you want me to talk to the manager?"

"No, I'm coming." He slammed the door of the Jeep. "I can't picture Pricilla here, that's all." He scanned the group of individual cabins circling the pothole-ridden drive and sighed. "Let's get this over with." He didn't like bringing Tennie here, especially after the glorious morning they had spent in the shower.

Tennie followed Reece to the office and smiled as he held the door open for her. Her smile buckled his knees, and he quickly glanced away from her.

The man behind the counter received all his attention. He was somewhere in his sixties, his receding hairline had met the collar of his shirt, a fat cigar was clamped between his smirking lips, and his gaze was riveted to Tennie's chest.

Reece stepped in front of Tennie and counted to ten. "We would like—"

"That will be twenty-nine dollars plus tax." He pushed a rusty key across the counter. "Cabin number three and the sheets were just washed." He flashed a toothless grin at Tennie and winked.

Reece saw red. "I'm going to—"

Tennie quickly stepped forward and took Reece's hand which was clenched into a tight fist. She didn't like the dirty little man behind the counter either, but knowing her family his chances of being an actor were the same as anybody else's in this town. "Excuse me, sir." She gently patted Reece's hand and prayed he would behave himself. "We don't want a room, we want to ask you a few questions."

The man shifted his cigar to the other corner of his mouth. "About what?"

"Tailpipe Taylor."

"Ah, the crazy old coot who got himself squashed by that truck?"

"Yes, that's him." Tennie sighed in relief as she felt Reece start to relax. "We're investigating his murder."

"Don't know nothing about no murder." He returned the rusty old key to its place under the counter. "Do know that I'm going to miss his business, though."

Reece pulled Tennie a few inches closer. "I gather Mr. Taylor was a regular?"

"Yep. He liked cabin number seven. Said it was his lucky cabin."

"How many times a month did Mr. Taylor visit your establishment?" Reece asked. His voice was thick with sarcasm that clearly went over the man's head.

"Tailpipe stopped by two, sometimes three times a week."

Tennie and Reece stared at each other in astonishment. What was Tailpipe, part jackrabbit? The man was seventy-two years old, for cripes sake. Tennie closed her mouth and tried to concentrate on the investigation. "Do you know Pricilla Stone?"

"Sure, everyone knows Pricilla."

"Was she Tailpipe's guest?" It sounded a lot better than asking this sleazy manager if Pricilla was the one Tailpipe was doing *the wild thing* with.

"Sometimes."

Reece's eyes narrowed and he pinned the man with a hard look. "Do you mean to tell us Tailpipe had more than one 'guest'?"

"Not at the same time." The man chuckled at the notion. "I don't think even Tailpipe had that kind of energy."

Tennie frowned at this latest development. "Who were the other guests?"

"Guest, ma'am." His gaze only momentarily fell to the front of Tennie's sweatshirt. "There was only one lady besides Pricilla."

"Who?" asked Reece and Tennie in unison.

"Don't know."

"I thought everyone in Little Lincoln knows everyone else," Reece said.

"We do, but the lady in question definitely wanted to keep her identity a secret."

"How do you mean?" asked Tennie.

"She always came with Tailpipe, dressed in big coats with hats pulled down over her face."

"You never saw her?"

"Nope. I couldn't tell you if she was old or young."

"Great," Reece muttered.

"But I have my theory."

"Which is?" asked Tennie.

"She has to be from around here, right? Why else would she hide her identity?"

Tennie mustered a half smile for his opinion, but she had already figured that one out. "Is there anything else you could tell us about her?"

The man scratched his bald head and thought. "Well there is one thing."

"What's that?" Tennie asked eagerly.

"She only came on Tuesday nights."

"Tuesday nights?"

"Every Tuesday night. You could set your watch by it. Every Tuesday night at seven-fifteen they pulled in and parked in front of cabin seven. Tailpipe would come over, pay the bill, and pick up the key. By nine o'clock they were long gone."

"Are you sure?"

The manager blew out a puff of smoke. "Yeah, positive."

———————❖———————

Tennie bit into her sandwich and moaned with ecstasy. It was after two and she was starved. She took a sip of iced tea and said to Reece, "So tell me finally what Ralph had to say."

He reached over their lunch and gently rubbed the dot of mayonnaise on her lip. She ate with the same gusto as she made love. "Ralph didn't have much to say. He seemed genuinely upset that Tailpipe was killed."

"I wonder why?" She had seen the heat that ignited in Reece's gaze and decided to behave herself or they were never going to make it out of Sadie's Diner without embarrassing themselves.

"Seems over the years, Ralph got comfortable with his medical problem and Pricilla's affair with Tailpipe. Ralph was the one who recommended Tailpipe in the first place, remember?"

"So?" She took another bite.

"Tailpipe wasn't a threat to the one thing Ralph holds dear, Pricilla's love. You see, it didn't matter how many times Pricilla and Tailpipe did *the wild thing*, she always came home to Ralph. She used Tailpipe's body, like I'm sure he used hers. It was all very civilized and meaningless." Reece picked up a french fry and waved it under Tennie's nose. "Pricilla loves Ralph and would never dream of leaving him for Tailpipe."

"Wouldn't Ralph be happy that Tailpipe is now out of the picture?"

"Just the opposite. Ralph is now scared that Pricilla is going to find someone else, maybe this time fall in love with her partner, and leave him."

Tennie chewed and thought. It looked like Ralph was in the clear. "Do you think Pricilla will go manhunting?"

"Who knows?" He ran the end of a french fry through a glob of ketchup and plopped it into his mouth. "I told Ralph it deserved him right if she did."

"You didn't!" Tennie cried. "How can you be so heartless?"

"I did it for his own good. I told him to get some professional help and conquer this fear of geese, or whatever it was that caused his condition. I said that if he was a man, and he really did love Pricilla as much as he claimed, then he ought to fight this fear and regain control of his life and his wife." Reece winked at Tennie. "I also hinted that Pricilla was a very sexy and dynamite lady that any man would be glad to have."

"You didn't!" Tennie chuckled. Reece was playing dirty pool to save a marriage. She never noticed this caring side of him before. She had always figured he would go out of his way to avoid other people's problems. Was he changing, or had she been blind all this time?

"Sure I did." He popped another ketchup-soaked

french fry into his mouth. "Have I told you how ravishing you look sitting there with two drops of mayonnaise christening the front of your sweatshirt?" He leaned in closer and whispered, "When we get back to the lodge, I'm going to see where else you might have dropped some food."

"Are you that hungry, Reece?" She knew exactly how the double entendre sounded.

"Famished."

She glanced down at his almost full plate and smiled. "There's a whole meal sitting in front of you."

"But, Tennie, love, I'm not hungry for food." His gaze lingered on her lips and the promises they made.

Reece rapped harder on the door. Tennie and he knew someone was inside, they could hear the music blaring and the curtains had moved the first time they had knocked. It was their third visit to Fanny's apartment and this time they weren't leaving until she talked to them.

Tennie and Reece took an instinctive step backward as the door opened. A woman around sixty-five or so stood there glaring. "I don't want any."

Reece jammed his foot into the doorway before the slamming door closed all the way. "Fanny Stone?" This was Ralph's meek and mild other sister? This woman buried under a pound of pancake makeup, cherry-red lipstick, and a muumuu splattered with huge orange hibiscus was Henrietta's sister?

"Who wants to know?" She held the door pressed against Reece's sneaker-clad foot.

He refused to show any pain. "I'm Reece Carpenter and this is Tennie Montgomery. We're investigating the death of Tailpipe Taylor."

Fanny's face paled under the makeup. "What's that got to do with me?"

Tennie smiled brightly and moved in closer. "Absolutely nothing, Ms. Stone." She nudged Reece aside and made direct eye contact with Fanny. "We understood that Tailpipe recently worked on your car."

"Well, yes." Her grip relaxed on the door. "The radiator had to be replaced."

"Oh, you poor dear," Tennie cried. "I know what you must have gone through. I once had to have a complete transmission job. If the worry and the expense weren't enough, the inconvenience would make you crazy."

Fanny blinked at the raving woman standing in front of her. "Well . . ."

"Did he do a good job?" Tennie asked. She waved her hands in disgust at the mere thought. "You hear stories about how mechanics take advantage of us women all the time." She moved closer to the door and inched her way inside. "You don't mind if we come in for a minute?" Before the astonished Fanny could reply, Tennie pressed on. "Tailpipe wasn't *that* kind of mechanic, was he?"

"No, of course not."

Reece quickly moved in behind Tennie and closed the door. The little minx was incorrigible, but effective. The calypso music was blasting out of the outdated stereo sitting in the corner of the sparsely furnished room. Fanny Stone was not living in the lap of luxury. Neat and tidy, yes; luxury, no.

"So you were satisfied with the work Tailpipe had done on your car?" Tennie asked. Her gaze scanned the room and landed on three brand-new dresses hanging on the back of the closet door. Fanny was living in a one-room apartment, if you didn't count the tiny bathroom and the closet. The kitchen, living room, and bedroom were all contained in a fourteen-by-twenty-four-foot room. The information she had received on Fanny must have been correct. Fanny was sixty-five, never married, and in February she had retired from her factory assembly job where she had been employed since her sixteenth birthday. For forty-nine years Fanny had sat in front of some machine and attached plastic tips to shoelaces. Thousands, millions, probably billions of shoelaces had passed through her aged hands. Tennie shuddered at the thought of what that could do to a person's mind. The words *serial killer* popped into her brain.

Her gaze slid back to the dresses. If Fanny was as strapped for money as she appeared, why were there three brand-new and outrageously expensive dresses wrapped in clear plastic hanging on her closet door?

"Not only was Tailpipe a very fine mechanic, he was also Little Lincoln's only mechanic." Fanny seemed to come out of her daze. "Are you questioning everyone who had their cars serviced by Tailpipe?"

"No, just a select few," Reece replied.

"May I be so bold as to ask why me?"

"Your car was seen a lot around Tailpipe's garage this past month."

"So, I just told you I had the radiator replaced."

"Most radiators would only take a day, maybe two, three tops. What was so special about yours?" asked Reece. He saw Tennie move closer to the Formica-topped kitchen table and the pile of papers there. He held Fanny's gaze.

"He didn't do the job right the first time," Fanny snapped.

"But you said Tailpipe was a great mechanic."

"I said he was a *good* mechanic and the *only* mechanic. I didn't say he was perfect." Fanny shifted her bulk and slapped her hand down on top of the brochures Tennie was reading. "I think it's time for you two to go."

Tennie slowly headed for the door. "Did you know Tailpipe was having an affair with your sister-in-law Pricilla?"

"Give me a break. Everyone knew that. It's old news, real old news." She opened the door.

Reece sighed. He was getting awfully tired of being thrown out of people's houses lately.

"Are you planning on going on a cruise?" asked Tennie. A person would have to be deaf not to hear the calypso music, or blind not to notice her ridiculous muumuu. Seeing the cruise brochures piled on her kitchen table was a stroke of luck.

"That's none of your business!" She held the door open wider and tapped her foot.

Reece walked passed her and smiled. Tennie came to a halt as two things struck her as peculiar. Where did Fanny's money for the cruise come from? The brochures advertised honeymoon getaways or lovers' retreats. Fanny wasn't planning on going alone. "I have one more question before I leave, Fanny."

Fanny only glared back at her.

"What do you do on Tuesday nights?"

Fanny turned pale. Her hand trembled violently as it clasped the door. "I sit in front of my thirteen-inch black-and-white TV and watch stupid game shows and even stupider sitcoms." Tears filled her sad-looking eyes. "It's the same thing I do night after night, year after year." The dam broke forth and tears streamed down her face. "Is there a law against that?"

Tennie felt like a heel and mentally kicked herself. She glanced helplessly at Fanny and had no idea what to say. "I'm sorry."

"Sorry." Fanny sniffed. "I don't need your sympathy. I did what I had to do when I quit school at sixteen to go to work in the factory so Ralph could go to trade school and sweet baby Henrietta could have new dresses and go to parties."

"You gave up your dreams for theirs?" Tennie's question was spoken softly.

"Of course I did. There was no other choice. Ralph was a boy, he was expected to learn a trade and support a family of his own one day. Henrietta was the baby of the family. Everyone catered to sweet, beautiful Henrietta." Her voice cracked with tension. "She never knew what it was like to work for ten hours straight and come home and listen to her baby sister tell her about the party she was going to that night, or about her latest beau. She never knew what it was like to work seven days a week for six months so her baby sister could walk down the aisle wearing a store-bought wedding dress." Fanny's entire body was shaking with rage. "Henrietta never knew what it was like to watch someone else marry the man she loved."

Tennie cautiously reached out. "Fanny?"

Fanny stiffened and swiped at the tears still pouring down her face. "Get out and don't you dare pity me."

Tennie hadn't meant to make Fanny cry. After they left, Reece pulled her into his arms and held her close. She was too softhearted not to be affected by such a showing of emotions. "Love?"

"Hmmm . . ." Tennie sniffled and started to search through her purse for a tissue.

"What are the chances that Fanny is one of the actresses?"

She glanced over her shoulder at the closed door. Doubt besieged her as a curtain moved in the window. Fanny was watching them. Damn if she hadn't fallen for the old-lady-in-the-muumuu-crying-her-eyes-out routine. She wiped away the last of the moisture in her eyes as she marched toward the Jeep. Boy, if her grandfather found out about this, she would never live it down.

TEN

Tennie clung to Reece's lips for a moment longer before reluctantly pulling back. "We really should go in and get ready for dinner."

A devilish smile spread across his face. Even after three nights in her bed he still couldn't get enough of her. "A shower right about now would be great."

Tennie blushed at the memories of their earlier shower that morning. Had she really been that depraved? That desperate? That pleading? She glanced at the wicked grin lighting up Reece's face and sighed. She guessed she had. "Separate showers this time?"

"No way, beautiful." He reached out and playfully tugged at her ponytail. "I promise not to let the faucet get in the way this time."

Their morning's shower had ended up in a wrestling match because she loved steaming hot showers while Reece preferred a temperature that guaranteed to leave on some of his skin. A bubble of laughter emerged from Tennie as she quickly jumped out of the Jeep. "First one in gets to set the water temperature." She sprinted for the entrance to the lodge, ignoring his shouts of outrage.

Reece yanked the keys out of the ignition and ran after her. He couldn't wait until he got her into a nice *warm* shower. He was going to teach her a lesson or two. His feet faltered for a second as uncontrollable desire rocked his body. He wrenched open the door and raced into the lobby. Damn if that little minx wasn't going to pay for this, and pay dearly. He ignored some startled glances and rounded the corner heading for the stairs. He was so busy looking ahead of him trying to spot Tennie that he failed to see who was standing directly in front of him. Reece crashed head-on into Tennie's back.

Tennie was thrown forward and if it wasn't for her uncle's quick reflexes she might have ended up spread-eagle on the lobby floor. She glared over her shoulder. "Reece!"

He had tried reaching for her shoulders as she went sailing, but only came up clutching air. "Tennie! Are you all right?"

"Yes, but no thanks to you." She straightened her sweatshirt and tugged the straps of her enormous purse up onto her shoulder, thankful that the mere weight of it hadn't sent her sprawling.

"Why did you stop?"

Tennie waved to the man standing next to her. "Don't you remember my uncle Colorado?" She smiled sweetly as Reece's mouth fell open. "The same uncle who was in jail for the murder of Tailpipe Taylor."

"You're out!" Reece sputtered.

"Observant as all hell, isn't he, Colorado?" Tennie purred. "One day he will make a fine detective, not as good as a Montgomery, but passable."

Reece frowned at Tennie and ignored Colorado's chuckle. The little minx was going to pay for that comment too. "Did you make bail?"

"Nope, they released me."

"Why?" Tennie and Reece asked at the same time. Reece glanced at Tennie and was happy to see she wasn't that far out in front of him. She hadn't any idea what was going on either.

"Seems the hydraulic lift specialist finally showed up, five days late, but he did manage to examine the lift."

"And?"

"The lift hadn't been tampered with. There were no signs of any foul play. They're ruling Tailpipe's death as a suicide."

"You're joking?" cried Tennie. There was no way Tailpipe's death was a suicide. No one in his right mind stood under a truck and let it slowly descend on him until there was nothing left except small squashed body parts. Someone murdered him as sure as her name was Tennessee Ellery Montgomery.

Reece looked around the lobby and noticed they were drawing a small crowd. He didn't mind the other family members trying to hear whatever Colorado had to say, but let them do it on their own time. Tennie and he would become the laughing stock of the family if they couldn't solve this mystery. After all, they were the best. "Colorado, let's go into the lounge area. I'm sure you could use a drink after everything you've been through." He expertly maneuvered them into the lounge and away from curious ears.

"That's the best idea I've heard all day." He smiled at the waitress and said, "Scotch, and you better make it a double."

Tennie said, "White wine, please."

Reece gave his order to the waitress and turned his attention back to Colorado. "You mean the police actually think Tailpipe committed suicide?"

"Don't rightly know what those two yokels think. All I know is they couldn't hold me any longer."

"Were you really seen outside of the garage the morning he was killed?" Tennie asked.

"Probably. I was walking down Main Street about that time." Colorado smiled at the waitress as she set his drink down in front of him. He picked it up and took a sip.

"What were you doing walking? Where was your car?"

"Emma Sue had followed me into Wellington that morning. The carburetor was misfiring again. Tailpipe had looked at it a couple of days before that, but he couldn't fix it. I had to take it to a dealership in Wellington."

"So your car's in Wellington?"

"Still is," Colorado said. "Utah is taking me out tomorrow to pick it up."

"So why didn't Emma Sue drop you at the cabin you were renting?" Reece asked.

"I was hungry, so I asked Emma Sue to take me to Sadie's. She dropped me off but refused to come in and have a meal with me. She was worried about gossip."

"After your meal, you walked from Sadie's back to the cabin, which took you past the garage?"

"Yep." Colorado took another sip of Scotch. "Five point two miles."

"That's a pretty good hike, Uncle."

Colorado swirled the ice in his drink. "Gives a man a lot of thinking time."

"So does sitting in a jail cell," Tennie muttered. She locked gazes with Colorado. "Want to tell us about Emma Sue?"

Ice cubes clinked against the side of his glass. "She has nothing to do with this."

"I think she does," Tennie said. "What were you doing sitting at her breakfast table wearing one of Tailpipe's old robes a couple days after his murder?"

"Suicide, Tennie. The police are ruling it suicide." He took another sip. "That means there was no murder and no mystery, so you can stop with the infernal questions."

"You and I both know Tailpipe didn't push the

button on the lift assembly and then jump back under Ralph's pickup, Colorado."

Colorado continued to stare into the depths of his glass. With a determined look he downed the remaining Scotch and placed the empty glass on the table. "Thanks for the drink, Reece. I have to be going now. Emma Sue will be joining us in a celebration dinner and I want to get cleaned up." He stood and walked out of the lounge.

Tennie frowned when she saw Aunt Maine and her two sons, Kentucky and Arizona, corner Colorado in the lobby. Colorado looked to be in for a long night of questions and answers. And he didn't seem too pleased.

"So, now what? Do we continue to investigate?" asked Reece.

"Of course. My family is notorious for throwing brick walls up. They want to see how many of us will take the easy way out and allow the local police to label the death a suicide." Tennie took a sip of her wine. "I smell a trap, Reece, a big fat Montgomery trap."

"How many do you think will take the bait?"

"Some." She put down her drink and lightly ran her fingers over the back of his hand. "The ones whose hearts weren't in it to begin with." A devilish gleam entered her eyes as she measured the distance between their table and the door. She nonchalantly reached for her purse.

Reece saw her intentions, and desire heated his blood. Her eyes had given her away. Within a flash he threw some money down on the table and dashed for the door. He heard Tennie mutter a word that was both lewd and exciting, depending on one's perspective. Taking the steps two at a time, he passed his startled-looking mother and his amused stepfather as they descended the stairs. "Hello, good-bye, no time to stop and chat." He sprinted up the remaining steps and ran down the hall.

Tennie was five steps behind him when she passed his mother and her uncle Utah. She smiled sweetly and said, "Nice day we're having," without breaking her stride.

Celeste and Utah looked at each other and grinned as Tennie shot out of sight. "Ah, love is in the air," whispered Utah. He bent and kissed his wife.

Celeste looked at the half-filled lobby. "We seem to be awfully early for dinner, dear."

Utah followed her gaze and grinned. "So it seems, precious, so it seems." He gently took her arm and turned her. There was a certain spring to his step as they retraced their way back to their room.

Tennie and Reece entered the dining room and noticed that almost everyone was enjoying dessert. Curious glances followed them as they made their way to a table. Tennie tried desperately to control the blush threatening to sweep her cheeks. She tilted up her chin and sat down next to her aunt Maine. "Sorry we're late."

It was all Reece's fault. First there was a race down

the hall and into the shower. It had been a tie; they had both stepped into the shower at the same instant. It hadn't mattered that Tennie had still been wearing her jeans and sneakers and Reece still had on his white briefs and one sock. It had been declared a tie and the clothes hadn't stayed on that much longer anyway. They would have made it to dinner on time even after the thoroughly satisfying shower, except for the flowers. Two dozen red roses had been the culprit. When Tennie opened the door to her room to get dressed, there on the dresser stood a crystal vase overflowing with the fragrant roses. Tears of happiness filled her eyes as she read the note sitting beside the vase. *I'm hoping this says 'I love you' better than I did the other night.* It had been signed with a capital R. She had looked up and seen Reece leaning against the doorjamb wearing nothing but a damp towel wrapped around his waist and a devastating smile. Needless to say they were very late for dinner.

"No problem, dear." Maine folded her napkin, pushed away her dessert plate, and frowned at the other two empty seats at the table. "It seems you're not the only ones."

Reece took the seat on the other side of Tennie and smiled at Edward Courtland, Maine's husband. The poor man had been stuck, more than likely, eating his entire meal, listening to his wife's constant whining. Of all the Montgomerys Maine was the only one who rubbed him the wrong way. The woman's whining was more irritating than someone running his fingers down a chalkboard. "Who else is missing?" He glanced around the dining room to see who hadn't showed up.

"Your mother and stepfather," replied Maine. "Edward and I took the liberty of eating our meal already, since we were unsure if anyone was going to join us."

"That's perfectly fine, Aunt Maine." Tennie tried to smooth her aunt's feathers. "We wouldn't dream of you waiting on us, would we, Reece?"

"No, of course not." Reece smiled pleasantly and glanced at a menu. "What would you recommend, Maine?"

"Well, the filet mignon was a bit tough tonight," Maine complained.

"Oh, hush, Maine. You know damn well the meat was perfectly done and so tender, it practically melted in your mouth." Indy and Pinky stopped by the table on their way out. "Your fangs probably need sharpening," said Indy. He gave a robust laugh as Maine sputtered.

Tennie glanced at Edward who was trying without too much success to hide his amusement. "Grandfather, stop teasing Auntie Maine."

Indy sighed as Pinky elbowed him in the side. "All right." He brushed a kiss across Tennie's cheek. "Glad to see you two finally made it down for dinner."

Tennie blushed.

Indy chuckled. "Here I was getting ready to send room service up to you."

Reece cleared his throat nervously and looked around to see if anyone had a shotgun pointed in his direction.

Indy had mercy on the pair and switched the subject. "By the looks of things I guess I'm still going to have to stop by the desk and order a tray sent up to Utah's room." He purposely nodded to two conspicuous empty chairs.

Maine moaned and waved her napkin in front of her. "Really, Father!"

Indy held the chair out for Maine to rise. "Why don't you and Edward join us in the lounge for drinks and see if you can convince me of that statement?" He glanced at Tennie and Reece and winked. Maine, Edward, and Pinky made their way out of the dining room. Indy stood by the table a moment longer and watched them leave before he said, "You two owe me one." He shuddered at the evening ahead. "A big one."

Forty-five minutes later Tennie and Reece stood in the lobby, trying to decide if they should join the family in the lounge, go outside for a walk, or Reece's personal choice, return to their rooms. Tennie laughed at another one of Reece's outrageous proposals and glanced around to make sure they weren't being overheard. She spotted Emma Sue sitting alone by a huge glass wall overlooking the distant mountains. "Reece, look." She nodded to Emma Sue who seemed deep in thought.

Reece grinned. The sooner they solved the case, the sooner he could have Tennie all to himself. "Want to go talk to her?"

Tennie was already halfway across the lobby floor. "Of course." She pulled up a chair across from Emma Sue and sat down. "Mind if we join you?"

Startled, Emma Sue nearly jumped. "No, please do."

Reece pulled up a chair. "Where's Colorado?" The lobby looked fairly deserted.

"In the lounge with his family." Emma Sue smiled at Tennie. "You must forgive me, dear, but there are so many of them that I needed a small break."

"We can be overpowering in numbers." Tennie relaxed. Emma Sue seemed able to hold her own with her family and the woman knew how to speak her mind. "Would you mind if Reece and I ask you a few questions?"

"No, of course not, dear. Colorado has been scaring everyone else off. He's very protective, you know."

Tennie raised an eyebrow at that understatement. "We noticed. Do you know they're classifying Tailpipe's death as a suicide?"

"Rubbish, pure rubbish." Emma Sue glanced between Tennie and Reece. "Tailpipe would no sooner kill himself than I would. The man loved life too much, or more accurately, the man loved himself too much."

"Did you know he was having an affair with Pricilla Stone?"

"I knew that years ago. Tell me something I don't know."

"Did you know he was seeing someone else too?"

Emma Sue nodded. "I figured as much. I think that affair was going on for about seven months."

"It didn't bother you?" Tennie asked.

"At first I was insulted, but then it hit me, as long as he was fulfilling his needs somewhere else he was leaving me alone."

"Why didn't you leave him?"

"And go where?" Emma Sue shook her head. "We never had children and my entire life has been dedicated to taking care of the house and him. Where would I go?" She looked at Tennie. "Do you realize how lucky you are? You have a career, you know a skill. If you had to, you could support yourself. You wouldn't hang on to a man out of desperation, would you?"

"Maybe if I loved him enough," Tennie said softly. Would she cling to Reece?

Emma Sue scowled. "Love has nothing to do with it. Tailpipe and I hadn't shared a bedroom in ten years. There was no love, Tennie, only mutual understanding. He understood that I would take care of him and I understood he would take care of me."

Tennie and Reece were silent for a moment while they digested that one. "Do you know of anyone who might have wanted to see Tailpipe dead?" Reece asked.

"No one," Emma Sue answered. "I've thought

about it a lot too. I can't think of a soul who would want to hurt him."

"Do you know what he did with the loan money?" Tennie asked.

"I didn't know nothing about the loan until the bank called me a couple days after the funeral."

"You have no idea what he did with the money?"

"No. The police searched the garage and I looked everywhere in the house. There is no money."

"How about outstanding debts?" Reece questioned.

"Oh, there were plenty of those all connected with the garage. I took care of the household expenses so they were all current."

Tennie sighed, they had hit another dead end. She liked Emma Sue and trusted her opinions, actress or no actress. "What's your opinion of Fanny Stone?"

"Fanny?" Emma Sue thought for a moment. "Fanny's a very reliable person. She worked for years and never cheated anyone that I know of. She goes to church every Sunday, usually with Henrietta and Stan. I don't want to sound like a gossiper but everyone knows she had a crush on Stan since the day Henrietta brought him home."

"We already knew that," Tennie reassured her.

"Then I guess you figured out she always has been jealous of Henrietta?"

"What about Henrietta? Did she ever confront Fanny?"

"Henrietta's too busy with her geese and being

jealous of everyone else around her to notice anything that's going on."

"Meaning?" Tennie was positive that Emma Sue was skirting a major issue.

"I don't really want to say. It would seem petty."

"Emma Sue, please," Tennie said. "We all know that Tailpipe was murdered. Don't you want to catch the murderer?"

Emma Sue hesitated.

"If not for Tailpipe, what about Colorado?" Reece said. "If it's proven that Tailpipe was actually murdered and didn't commit suicide then the finger points directly back to Colorado again."

"It's Stan," Emma Sue said softly.

"What about Stan?" Tennie and Reece shared a quick glance.

"He's"—she looked decidedly embarrassed—"made a pass at me a couple of times."

"What exactly do you mean by a 'pass'?" asked Tennie when she found her voice. Why anything still surprised her on this case she didn't know. But making a pass at Emma Sue was like making a pass at Aunt Bee on *Mayberry*.

"Who's making a pass?" demanded Colorado, who had sneaked up on them undetected.

All three jumped in surprise. "Do you have to creep up on people like that, Uncle?" cried Tennie as soon as she could unlodge her heart from her throat.

"Don't change the subject, Tennie," Colorado ordered. His ruthless glare settled on Reece. "I want to know who's making a pass at Emma Sue?"

"It's not me, sir," Reece said. He glanced at Tennie and winked. "My heart is already spoken for."

Colorado glanced between a blushing Tennie and Reece. "Is that a declaration, son?"

"Yes, sir." Reece chuckled as Tennie sank lower into the chair and covered her eyes with her hands. If she thought they were going to hide their feelings from her family she had another think coming. Besides being so blatantly obvious, their love wasn't something he wanted to hide. The entire world should now about it.

Colorado held out his hand to Emma Sue. "Then I think I need to return a favor, Reece, and buy you a drink. Would you and Tennie like to join us in the lounge?"

"It would be our pleasure, sir." Reece held out his hand to Tennie who ignored it and stood up on her own. He watched Colorado and Emma Sue walk toward the lounge. "I take it you're a little miffed?"

"Miffed?" Tennie repeated. "The Boston Strangler was miffed. The Son of Sam was miffed." She jabbed her finger into his chest. "I, Mister-know-it-all, am royally furious. Do you have any idea what's going to happen once we enter the lounge?"

"Colorado buys us a drink?"

"*Everyone* will buy us a drink. They will think—"

Her mind went blank for a moment. She couldn't rightly tell Reece that her family would be picking out churches and wedding invitations.

"That we are in love?" Reece questioned.

"Well, yes, but . . ."

Reece took pity on her and hugged her tight. He couldn't stand to see such a distressing look on her gorgeous face. "Don't worry, love, we won't let them bully us into anything we aren't ready for."

Tennie relaxed and gently caressed his jaw. He had understood. Teasingly, she said, "Well if they do, you have only yourself to blame!"

Reece quickly kissed her and ushered her into the lounge.

A loud cheer went up as they made their way over to Colorado and Emma Sue. Reece protectively put his arm around Tennie. He looked at Colorado and said, "I see you didn't waste any time."

Colorado raised his glass. "Hell, son, we thought we'd never get you two together."

"What do you mean, together?" Tennie asked. She glanced around the room at all the smiling faces and frowned. Her intuition was screaming that a trap had been sprung, and she was caught in the middle of it.

Someone handed her a glass of champagne and Grandfather Indy shouted, "A toast!" Glasses were raised throughout the room.

"Wait!" Tennie cried. "Would someone please tell me what's going on here?"

Reece glanced at the glass that had magically appeared in his hand. "Correction, tell *us* what's going on." He had expected to field a couple of questioning comments, not to be the guest of honor.

Everyone turned to Grandmom Pinky, who stood up and raised her glass. "This was all my doing, dears."

"What's all your doing? And put down that glass, Grandmom, you shouldn't be drinking in your condition."

"I guess it's confession time." Pinky smiled at Indy as he came and stood beside her. "This reunion had a dual purpose. One was the mystery, but the second was more important. We wanted to get you and Reece together and expose what had been clearly obvious for the past two years."

"You've been matchmaking!" Tennie cried, horrified.

Pinky cleared her throat and took a sip of champagne. "Afraid so, dear. We all knew you and Reece were perfect for each other, but you both were too stubborn to see it. We were afraid that this year would be another repeat of the past."

"So you made us partners," Reece said. It wasn't a question, just a statement of the facts.

"Yes."

Reece and Tennie looked at Indy. "There's nothing wrong with her heart, is there?" Tennie asked.

Indy put his arm around Pinky. "Only that it's sometimes too big, and tends to butt into other people's business." He kissed Pinky's cheek and his voice got all husky. "But it's pure gold, and I wouldn't have her any other way."

Tennie glanced at Reece. There was no way she could yell at her grandparents. They had meant well, and it had given her a chance to fall in love with Reece. All things considered, she probably owed them one hell of a thank you. "What do you think? Should we let them off the hook?"

Reece smiled and hugged Tennie closer. He was personally sending everyone in the room a gold-engraved thank-you note. "It's your call, love."

Tennie slowly shook her head at her grandparents and the surrounding crowd. She noticed her parents and Reece's watching closely. "We forgive you this time." A loud cheer erupted. "Wait! I'm not finished yet." The room settled back down. "What happens between Reece and me will be our own business from now on. Is that clear?" She glanced around the room at the nodding heads. "We won't be pushed into anything we aren't ready for." The heads continued to nod. "I love you all, but I'm warning you, butt out or else." The nodding heads jerked in unison. Tennie's *"or elses"* were notorious throughout the family.

"Tennie, dear," Pinky said. "We only wanted to get you two together. Once we got you there, it's up to you to do the rest." She raised her glass. "Can we at least toast your current happiness and a well-executed plan on our parts?"

Tennie raised her glass and Reece followed. "On

one condition," Reece said. All eyes turned to him. "That nothing more on the matter is mentioned." He could tell Tennie was feeling the pressure.

The glasses were raised and a chorus of "To happiness" filled the room. Reece took a sip of his champagne and turned to Colorado. "So how is the fishing in these parts?"

It took Tennie twenty minutes before she was able to relax. She got a refill of champagne muttering something about "*only in the Montgomerys*" and slid up behind Reece. He was talking to Uncle Colorado. She slipped her arm around Reece's waist and grinned over his shoulder at her uncle.

"So, Reece," Colorado said, "who is closer to solving the mystery, you or Tennie?"

Tennie stuck out her tongue at her uncle as Reece said, "You're forgetting, Colorado, we are partners." He reached behind him and gave her a quick squeeze. He had missed her these past minutes, but he knew she needed some breathing space.

"Oh, bologna," sputtered Colorado. "One of you has to be closer."

Reece put his arm around Tennie's shoulder as she moved next to him. "It doesn't matter anyway."

"Why the bloody hell not?"

"The reason it doesn't matter is because I was going to allow her to win this year anyway." He blinked in surprise as the entire room grew utterly quiet and still. He could have been transported to an E. F. Hutton commercial for all he knew. He turned to Tennie and realized his mistake instantly. She looked ready to blow up.

Tennie sucked in a breath and whispered one word that was heard clear across the room. *"Allow?"*

ELEVEN

"Now, Tennie, I didn't mean that the way it sounded," explained Reece.

"No?" Her glare was icier than a bobsled run and twice as deadly. "How exactly did you mean that?"

Reece felt the sweat break out on his palms. He was a dead man if he didn't watch his step. He flashed what he hoped was a boyish smile. "Tennie, love, you know how we fought the other years?"

"So?"

"This year, before I came here, I decided I wasn't going to really try to solve the mystery. I wasn't going to fight you, I was going to allow you to win."

"Are you saying that I couldn't have done it unless you so graciously backed off?" Her teeth were aching from being clamped together so tightly.

Reece glanced around looking for support and found none. "That's not what I said Tennie, stop putting words in my mouth."

"There's something in your mouth, Reece, and it isn't words. It looks more like a size-ten shoe." Tennie very carefully placed her glass on the small table in front of her. The temptation to hurl it against some wall was frightening. "You don't think I could solve this case without you, do you?"

"I didn't say that," Reece snapped. This was going too far. Here he was going to be a gentleman and allow her the victory and she turns into a raving shrew. Talk about gratitude.

"But you insinuated it!" Tennie shouted. "Do you know what you are?" Without allowing him to catch his breath she continued, "You're a fat-headed, conceited, arrogant, egotistical—"

"I get the picture!"

"I haven't even gotten started yet."

"For two cents, Tennie, I'll solve the damn mystery myself."

"You and what Montgomery?" The entire room held its breath as the gauntlet was thrown down.

"That does it!" Reece yelled. He was too upset to think clearly. In a voice as hard as steel he bit out, "I'll solve this damn mystery before you, or my name isn't Reece *Carpenter*."

Tennie angled up her chin and glared. "In your dreams, Carpenter. This year the victory will be won by a Montgomery—me!"

"This is from a woman who loses her keys in her purse, can't find her clothes in her own room, and so far has misplaced three pairs of sunglasses since we've been here. *You* expect me to believe that you will find a killer before me?"

Tennie took a threatening step forward.

Colorado read the murderous look in his niece's eye and reached out and took her arm. "Now, Tennie, don't go doing something you'll regret."

"I already regret doing a lot of things I've done recently." She shook off Colorado's hand. "Thanks for the party, everyone. I had a wonderful time." She snatched up her purse and headed for the door. "Sorry I can't stay longer. I need to get up early in the morning. It seems I have a murder to solve." She shot Reece one last parting glare. "That is, if I can find my way back to my own room." She stormed out of the lounge with her chin held high.

Reece watched the empty doorway for a full minute before he realized she wasn't coming back. She had walked out on him. She had walked out on them. Tennie had let something as trivial as who solved the murder come between them. There was absolutely nothing left for him here. He glanced around the room. Everyone was waiting for him to say something, anything. Maybe there was one thing left, the mystery. Tennie was a Montgomery, and everyone knew the Montgomerys loved to throw in brick walls and curveballs. Maybe that's what Tennie wanted him to do, go home to nurse his broken heart and allow her to solve the mystery. Tennie had made one fatal flaw in her reasoning. He was a Carpenter, and Carpenters never quit. He raised his glass high, cleared his throat, and gave a toast. "May the best detective win!"

Tennie pulled some more junk out of her purse and dumped it onto the hood of the Jeep. She had been standing in the parking lot for five minutes now, digging through her purse looking for the keys to the Jeep.

"Lose these?"

Her gaze followed the set of keys dangling from Reece's fingers and slowly swaying in front of her face. "I see you resorted to your old tricks, Reece." She held out her hand. "What's next—disconnecting my spark plug wires like I did to you last year?"

"No, I was planning on giving the keys back to you at breakfast, but since you didn't show up . . ." The keys landed in her palm. "I found them in the pocket of the jeans I wore yesterday."

She dropped the keys into her coat pocket and started to reload her purse. The morning was wasting. The sooner she could get into town to beg, plead, or literally beat the answers out of everyone connected with this case, the sooner she could solve the murder, declare victory, and get back to Iowa where she planned to pull the blanket up over her head and pretend this entire reunion never happened.

Tennie had no idea what to say to Reece. She could probably shout a couple of curses that would send him into cardiac arrest, but she discovered something last night as she paced around in her room. All those horrible things she had said last night in the lounge had hurt her more than they had hurt him. She couldn't deal with any more pain this morning, the tears were too close. Reece was too close. She wanted to throw herself into his arms and kiss him until her appetite returned. She picked up the packed purse and walked around Reece to the side of the Jeep. She had to get away now before she did something incredibly stupid. Without saying a word she unlocked the Jeep and got in. The engine barely roared into life before she threw it into gear and tore out of the parking lot.

Reece stood in the middle of the lot with his hands jammed into his coat pockets and watched as the Jeep disappeared around the curve. His heavy sigh broke the morning's peacefulness as he walked toward his rental car.

Tennie kept her eyes closed and her feet propped up on the seat across from her as Reece walked into Sadie's Diner. She knew it was him because she had seen his car pull into the lot a moment ago. She had been sitting in the last booth for an hour now, drinking endless cups of coffee, and resting. She had spent the morning running up and down the aisles in a food store, following Henrietta trying to get some answers from her. No, she didn't know anything more. No, Tailpipe didn't seem to be the type to commit suicide;

it must have been an accident. No, Fanny didn't have any boyfriend and she certainly didn't have any money for fancy cruises. Yes, Stan disliked Tailpipe for years, and no, she didn't know why.

The sound of Reece's footsteps stopped at the booth next to her. She listened to his smooth voice thank the hostess and the slight crackling of vinyl as he sat down. Great, Mr. Sherlock Holmes of the modern world was either following her or he had the same idea. Pricilla's shift was scheduled to end in a matter of minutes.

"Reece! I knew you couldn't keep away from me," Pricilla purred. She fluffed her hair and smoothed the pink uniform over her ample hips. "What will it be, sweetcakes?"

Reece chuckled for the first time that day. Pricilla could lighten anyone's mood. "Only coffee. I'm not very hungry."

Pricilla glanced at Tennie in the next booth. "Seems to be a lot of that going around today." She dropped her pad into the pocket of her apron. "I'll be right back with your coffee."

Reece watched her walk away before turning his attention on Tennie. She hadn't eaten! He hadn't been too worried this morning when she failed to show up for breakfast, but now he was concerned. For Tennie to pass up food twice in one morning was unprecedented. Either she was sick, or she was taking this war of the sleuths to heart. The last thing he wanted to do was to hurt her. All he had wanted to do was to eliminate the competition between them and see where it led. He now knew where it led, right into the biggest mess of his life. He was in love with a woman who wouldn't even speak to him. Great! This was his reward for trying to be a nice guy.

Pricilla set a cup down in front of him and poured the coffee. "Are you sure I can't get you something else?"

"You can do me one favor, Pricilla."

"What's that?" She placed a small silver pitcher filled with cream by the cup.

"If you have a few minutes when your shift is done, I could use some company."

Pricilla's shrewd glance traveled between him and the woman pretending to be asleep in the back booth. "I already told Tennie that I'd join her for a cup of coffee. Why don't you join us and you both can ask the questions? I hate to repeat myself and the rest of your family has been driving me bananas. Half the time I feel like a parrot."

Reece glanced at Tennie. She hadn't moved a muscle. "What makes you think I want to ask you questions, Pricilla?"

"Because, sweetcakes"—she rechecked her hair—"if I honestly thought you wanted something more, I'd punch out my time card and be in that booth with you faster than you could say Rumpelstiltskin."

He laughed. "You're incorrigible, Pricilla."

"Hell no, Reece." She winked suggestively. "Just plain old scrumptious."

Reece was still chuckling as she walked away. He stopped when Tennie stood up and placed a couple of bills down on her table. "Where are you going?"

"I have to see a man about a horse." She put on her jacket and started to walk away.

"What about Pricilla?" Reece asked.

"Tell her I had to leave, something came up." She dug her keys out of her purse and lightly tossed them up into the air. "I don't have all day to wait around. I have a murder to solve." She inched up her chin and walked out of the diner.

Reece stared out the window and frowned as Tennie's Jeep drove from the parking lot. The day kept getting better and better. Hell, and it wasn't even noon yet.

Pricilla placed her coffee cup down on his table and slid in the booth. She glanced at the booth Tennie had just vacated and then at Reece's expression. She picked up a packet of sugar substitute and dumped it into her coffee. "Reece, Reece"—she gave a couple of little clicking noises with her tongue—"what have you done?"

"Me? What makes you think I did anything?"

"Because when a woman's as upset as Tennie, a man has to be behind it." She stirred her coffee and sipped. "Why don't you tell Aunt Pricilla all about it."

Reece glanced up from the depths of his coffee and blurted out the first thing that came to his mind. "I'm in love with her."

Pricilla chuckled and gently patted his hand. "I already figured that one out the last time you two were in here. Tell me something I don't know."

Tennie pressed both her hands around the hot cup from her Thermos and continued to watch the golden eagle soar. He was breathtaking in his simplicity. Why couldn't life be like that, simple? The late afternoon sun was slowly descending behind the mountains in the west and the early spring cold had returned. She was sitting on the same outcrop of rocks she had found the other day, contemplating what to do now. The lodge was brimming with family members all curious as to what was happening between her and Reece. Five minutes back in the place had shown her she wouldn't find peace and quiet there. She had persuaded the kitchen to fix her a Thermos of hot coffee and had headed for the only sanctuary she knew, the mountains. The one other person who knew of this place was Reece, and he wasn't likely to come looking for her. She could have stayed in Little Lincoln, but it would have been a waste of time. She had already figured out who killed Tailpipe.

She had solved the mystery, first. So why wasn't she jumping for joy and shouting it to every member of her family who would listen? Why wasn't she rubbing Reece's nose in it instead of sitting on a lonely hunk of earth watching a lone eagle look for his dinner?

After she left the diner she went over to the beer distributor and had a nice chat with Ralph Stone. He had been everything Reece had claimed he was: Meek, intelligent, and extremely unhappy. She had been ready to call it another wash when Ralph unknowingly supplied the vital clue. Stan Marino bowled every Tuesday night. In a matter of minutes, Tennie had the entire mystery solved.

She also had realized she was now stuck between the proverbial rock and a hard place. If she went flying back to the lodge and claimed the victory, it would probably ruin any chance of her and Reece having a future. If she kept quiet and allowed Reece to solve the mystery, she would be no better than he and she would never be able to face herself in a mirror again.

Tennie took a sip of the hot coffee and smiled as the eagle made a dive for his dinner. At least someone had an appetite. She hadn't eaten anything all day and her coffee tolerance was about maxed out.

She used the back of her sleeve to wipe at the tears clouding her vision. She had missed Reece today something terrible. When he had walked into Sadie's, it had taken every ounce of fortitude she possessed to walk away. She missed his teasing laughter, his gentle touches, and the deep huskiness of his voice when he was excited. She missed his slow hot kisses and the way his rough jaw brushed against hers.

More tears blurred her vision as she dumped the remaining coffee on the ground. If she was such a great detective and could apply deductive reasoning to solving crimes, why couldn't she reverse the process and figure a way out of this? There had to be a way to show Reece what a great detective she was, and win his respect without jeopardizing their newly found love.

Tennie stood up and dusted off the backside of her jeans. She picked up the empty Thermos and headed back to the lodge. She was tired of everyone else getting the happily-ever-afters. They deserved one of their own, and by hell she was going to see that they got one, or her name wasn't Tennessee Ellery Montgomery.

It was after midnight, the witching hour, and Reece paced his room like some caged wild animal. He couldn't believe he had been that stupid. How could he have been that conceited as to think he would allow Tennie to solve this year's mystery? How could he have hurt the woman he loved that much? It had all seemed so simple back in San Francisco. Now it was a black hole of a nightmare sucking him in deeper.

Pricilla had been appalled when he told her what had happened. She said he was lucky to escape with his life, and manhood, intact. When Pricilla asked if Tennie was that bad of a detective, he had cried "Of course not!" Pricilla's next question had thrown him for a loop when she asked, "So what makes you so sure that she wouldn't have solved the mystery before you?"

It had been a long time before he could work up

the courage to answer Pricilla truthfully. He hadn't been sure at all. Tennie was every bit as good of a detective as he was. The first year he won the reunion mystery, it had been a fluke. Tennie had been working in her relaxed, laid-back style, mixing the mystery with quiet get-togethers with her family. He on the other hand had been pulling out every stop to solve the mystery first. He had struck while Tennie was unaware of the danger and with sheer perseverance he solved the murder first. The next year he knew Tennie would have her guard up and he had been ready for her. He combated her intelligence with tricks; she had surprised him by using some ingenious tricks of her own, and even then he had only won the victory by mere minutes. This year, if he were truly honest with himself, she might have pulled it off. So instead of competing against her, he would allow her to win. Even with all her unorthodox style, mass disorganization, and living in some hick town of Hogs Hollow, Tennie could match him any day of the week.

Now what was he supposed to do?

He couldn't very well go in there and beg Tennie's forgiveness and then say, "Oh, by the way, I know who killed Tailpipe." Tennie would rip out his heart and flush it down the john. He couldn't keep his mouth shut and allow Tennie to solve the mystery, because then he would be as bad as she thought he was. He loved her too much to do that.

Reece stared at the interconnecting door and wondered for the hundredth time if the manager had sent someone up to fix it. He hadn't noticed any signs that someone had gotten around to it. The brass knob still looked the same. His fingers gently touched it. Tennie was on the other side. Lord how he missed her today. When he'd returned to the lodge, the Jeep had been in its usual place, but Tennie was nowhere around. She hadn't shown up for dinner or joined in any of the family get-togethers afterward in the lounge or lobby. Concerned, he had ordered room service to send up a tray to her room and had discreetly tipped the bellboy for a full report on what she had eaten. He was rewarded with the glowing report that every plate, bowl, and glass came back empty. Either a lumberjack had taken up residence in Tennie's room, or her appetite had returned to normal. Was that a good sign?

Reece undressed and turned off the light. It was too late tonight to do anything. Tennie was probably asleep by now. If he was such a great detective and could apply deductive reasoning to solving crimes, why couldn't he reverse the process and figure a way out of this? There had to be a way to show Tennie that he thought she was a great detective, and win back her love. He was tired of everyone else having happy endings. They deserved one of their own, and by hell he was going to see that they got one, or his name wasn't Reece Sinclair Carpenter.

Tennie glared at her brother. "Would you be serious for a minute, Montana. I'll explain it to you again."

Montana finished off a stack of pancakes swimming in maple syrup while his kid sister went on and on about who killed Tailpipe, or more accurately who pushed the fatal button on the hydraulic lift that morning. He wiped his mouth and then downed his entire glass of orange juice as she finished the story for a second time. "You don't say."

"I do say," Tennie snapped. Her breakfast was still sitting in front of her only half eaten and getting cold. If she didn't have to repeat everything twice for Montana, her poor stomach wouldn't be rumbling. The brilliant idea on how to solve her problem came to her late last night, about the same instant a nervous-looking bellhop delivered a tray loaded down with food. She made a mental note to thank Indy and had dug into the food while rerunning her plan through her mind. It was perfect. It would solve all her problems. She would tell Montana who killed Tailpipe and allow him to claim the victory. She wouldn't be beating Reece, and she wouldn't be allowing Reece to beat her. She glanced across the dining room at Reece and his stepfather, Utah. They seemed to be in a heated discussion about something. She turned her attention back to Montana. "So when are you going to call the family together and announce who the murderer is?"

"I'm not." He reached over and swiped a strip of bacon from her plate.

"Why not?" Tennie cried. He had to do it. It was her only chance at happiness.

"Because I didn't solve the mystery, you did." He smiled and waved to Sue Ellen and the boys as they all came trooping into the dining room. "Besides"—he stood up and dropped a bill big enough to cover both of their breakfasts and then some onto the table—"I have other plans for the day." He brushed a soft kiss against Sue Ellen's cheek and took the infant carrier containing Galveston out of her hands.

Tennie frowned at the treacherous lot. "Where are you going?" They had no right to look so happy.

"Dad's taking us to a real ghost town," Austin said.

"There's gold there," added Dallas importantly.

Houston grinned and gave his version as to what the most important thing in a ghost was with one word, "Casper!"

Sue Ellen laughed and lovingly ran her fingers through her son's hair. "Did you want to come with us, Tennie?"

"No, you guys go exploring for the day. I have something more important to do." She glared at her brother. "I have to find someone else since my own brother won't do it for me."

"What won't you do?" Sue Ellen asked. She had never known Montana to refuse his sister anything, then again she never remembered Tennie asking for any favors. "We could postpone the trip until tomorrow."

"No," Tennie said. "You guys run along." She saw Sue Ellen hesitate and forced a brilliant smile.

"I mean it, Sue Ellen. Get going, everything's fine." She kept the smile in place as the boys and Sue Ellen headed back out, then she turned to her brother who still stood by the table. "Everything that is, except for my future."

"He's right over there. Why don't you go on over and tell him you solved the case."

"He'll hate me."

"Then he wouldn't be worth your love, would he?" Montana bounced the carrier lightly. "I think you might be misjudging him, Tennie. He seems like an okay guy to me."

"Of course he's an okay guy! Do you think I would love him if he wasn't?" She glanced across the room and watched as Utah burst out laughing and Reece turned a dull shade of red.

"No, I think you're just going about this all wrong." Montana shifted his son to his other hand. "Then again, you are a Montgomery."

She pulled her curious gaze off the far table and back to her brother. "What's that got to do with anything?"

"Montgomerys are notorious for never doing anything the easy way." He ambled out of the room, leaving Tennie to ponder that.

Across the room Utah hooted with laughter. "You want me to do what, son?"

"Just call a meeting with Indy, Pinky, and a few other Montgomerys and say you solved the mystery."

"But that would be cheating." Utah finished off

his coffee. "You're the one who solved it. You call the meeting."

"If I do that, Tennie will hate me for life." The idea to have Utah solve the crime had come to him somewhere around three o'clock in the morning. It was perfect, or at least it seemed that way until Utah refused to cooperate. Now what in the hell was he supposed to do? Beg every Montgomery to take credit for solving the mystery of the murder for him, until one agreed?

TWELVE

Tennie stood back and watched as everyone crowded into the lounge. Tonight was the night. The murderer was going to be revealed. She turned to North Carolina, who seemed more interested in checking the mirror to make sure her makeup was on right than the upcoming events. "Are you sure you have it straight now?" It had taken her two hours this afternoon to coach her through the entire investigation.

"If you explain it one more time, Tennie, I'm leaving."

"But what if they ask you questions on how you figured out certain parts?"

"Don't worry, I'll tell them it's a trade secret." North applied another coat of ruby-red lipstick and snapped the compact closed.

"Are you ready?"

"Let's get this show on the road. Jake's taking us out dancing later." She sauntered into the lounge.

Tennie glanced down at her outfit. It was the last new outfit she had brought with her. The skirt was yards and yards of flowing sheer material printed with brown, rust, orange, and gold seashells. It ended a few inches above her ankles and the simple rust-colored pumps she was wearing. The large open-weave rust-colored sweater ended at midthigh and gave enticing glimpses of the gold-colored chemise she wore underneath. She had left her hair long and unbound and she had even dug out some jewelry from the bottom of her suitcase. Tennie felt feminine and sexy as she walked into the crowded lounge.

Her glance immediately shot to Reece. He looked incredibly handsome in his suit. Lord, how she'd missed him.

Reece pulled his hungry gaze away from Tennie and gave South Carolina a nudge. "Go ahead. Do you remember everything I told you?"

"Of course I do. You told me enough times." She moved to the center of the room. "May I have your attention!" She smiled as everyone stopped talking. "I'm sure you all know why I called you here. I . . ." She held out her hand to North. "I mean, *we* have solved the mystery this year."

Tennie frowned. What was going on? North was the one who was supposed to solve the mystery.

Reece frowned. What was going on? He had just spent the whole afternoon coaching South through the entire investigation.

North and South Carolina hugged each other and

grinned. They both waved to Jake, as he stood in the back of the room, looking proud. "Tailpipe Taylor was *not* murdered," North declared.

A murmur went through the room.

"Tailpipe Taylor did *not* commit suicide," South declared.

"Did the truck accidentally fall on him?" asked Arizona. He joined in on the laughter surrounding him. Everyone knew the twins couldn't watch *Murder She Wrote* without becoming hopelessly confused.

"Not, exactly," North explained. "Everyone knew that Pricilla was having an affair with the victim, Tailpipe Taylor." She pointed to Pricilla.

Pricilla looked both thrilled and embarrassed by all the attention. She was still acting her part and had shown up at the lodge, wearing a pink dress that not only highlighted her hair but caused a wicked gleam in her husband Ralph's eye. The man had looked utterly speechless and hopelessly in love.

"You would think that Pricilla's husband would have done poor Tailpipe in." South pointed to Ralph. "But he didn't."

Tennie breathed a sigh of relief. For a minute there she thought North had forgotten everything she told her. She glanced at the twins and realized they had moved. She didn't know which was which. Tennie came closer to the twins in case one of them needed coaching. She wondered how South Carolina had solved the mystery. Had North gone back to their room and told her everything that she had said?

"Tailpipe was not only two-timing his poor wife, sweet Emma Sue"—one of the twins waved to the darling woman clinging to Colorado's hand—"but, he was also cheating on Pricilla."

A murmur of surprise went through the room, and Reece could tell who knew about the other woman and who didn't. He moved closer to the twins in case one of them needed further coaching.

"Tailpipe met with this woman every Tuesday night at the After Six Motel." North looked at Tennie and winked. South looked at Reece and winked. In unison they said, "Tuesday nights just happened to be Stan Marino's bowling night."

Everyone glanced at an obstinate-looking Stan and then at the woman sitting beside him. Henrietta was starting to cry, but Stan showed no sign of shock. "Henrietta has always been jealous of Pricilla and her carefree lifestyle. So when the opportunity came up to taste what sinful pleasures Pricilla was experiencing, she grabbed hold of it and started meeting Tailpipe every Tuesday night."

Tennie glanced around the room to see how everyone was taking this. She knew Montana had already heard this story, along with Kentucky, Edward, and Maine. North Carolina had been her last hope. Pinky and Georgia looked a little miffed that the case had been so easy that North and South Carolina could solve it.

"Fanny, who has always been in love with her sister Henrietta's husband, Stan, grew suspicious and followed her one Tuesday night. Imagine her surprise when the trail led to a sleazy motel room."

Reece moved in closer. Tennie was about ten feet away and looking more breathtaking every minute. He wished the twins would stop being so dramatic and spill it out.

"Instead of confronting the lovers, she ran to Stan and revealed the shocking truth. She had been hoping Stan would divorce Henrietta, but instead Stan had another plan. He used Fanny's love against her. He told her to blackmail Tailpipe and they would use the money for their own honeymoon after he divorced Henrietta."

One of the twins turned to Fanny and asked, "How could you blackmail your own sister?"

"He told me he loved me!" Fanny wailed. "He said the courts would give her everything and there wouldn't be anything left for our golden years." She started to cry into a lace hankie.

"Henrietta became hysterical when she learned about the blackmail. She didn't know how Stan was going to react so she convinced Tailpipe to take out a five-thousand-dollar loan and she had promised she would pay it back." The twins glared at Stan. "Only Stan cut off the household money and Henrietta was now penniless. She couldn't give Tailpipe the money to make the payments."

Tennie moved closer to Reece. If she closed her eyes and concentrated, she could pick up the exciting scent of his after-shave. Who cared about the drama unfolding in front of her? She wanted Reece.

"Tailpipe and Henrietta started to fight constantly about the money. Fanny still was threatening Henrietta because Stan hadn't left her yet. Stan sat back enjoying the show, because he knew that once Emma Sue heard about the loan it would be the last straw and she would leave Tailpipe, giving Stan the chance of a lifetime to declare his love for her."

Reece chuckled as Henrietta and Fanny glared at Emma Sue. Damn, they were great actresses. Colorado protectively drew Emma Sue closer. Reece moved around Florida and stopped directly behind Tennie. The exotic scent of sandalwood teased his senses.

"The morning Tailpipe was killed, Henrietta visited his garage." The twins grinned as a murmur went through the room. "You fought again, didn't you, Henrietta?"

She sniffled into a tissue. "He said he'd tell Stan unless I came up with the whole five thousand dollars. He said something about the bank threatening to take his house unless he paid up."

"So you killed him?"

"No!" Henrietta cried. "He was working on Ralph's truck and he said he was telling Stan that night." She sobbed harder into the tissue.

"So you pushed the lift button?"

"I didn't mean to! I got mad and swung my purse at him." She blew her nose. "The purse missed him, but hit the button by mistake. The button jammed and Tailpipe started screaming that his shirt was caught and couldn't get out. He was screaming something about a button, but I don't know nothing about lifts. By the time I found the right button, it was too late. Tailpipe wasn't screaming anymore.

"I was in a daze when I stepped out of the garage and saw Stan standing there. He called me a murderer." She shuddered. "I told him I didn't do it on purpose, that it was an accident, but he laughed and said the police would never believe it. He told me to go home and not to say nothing to nobody unless I wanted to spend the rest of my life behind bars." She cried harder and wailed, "I can't go to prison. They won't allow my geese there."

North and South Carolina confronted Stan. "You knew all along it was an accident, but you couldn't pass up the golden opportunity to implicate Uncle Colorado when you saw him walking by the garage that morning, could you?"

Stan folded his arms across his chest and smiled. "I didn't do anything wrong. The police were looking for anyone seen near the scene of the crime, and I happened to mention Colorado was there."

The twins turned to their grandparents. "So you see, there wasn't a murder at all. Tailpipe's death was accidental."

Indy and Pinky politely applauded. "Bravo, girls. You did an excellent job." They glanced around the room and smiled. They knew that almost everyone in the room had already solved the mystery, but had kept quiet hoping Tennie or Reece would capture the victory.

Reece moved in closer to Tennie and placed a hand on her arm as excited conversation broke out across the room. Everyone was either trying to congratulate the twins or find out who the actors really were. "Do you have a minute?"

Tennie glanced over her shoulder at Reece. She had noticed the way South Carolina kept looking at him during the speech. Reece had coached South as she had coached North. He had known what happened and refused to claim the victory. "For you?" She smiled up at him and softly said, "I might have longer than that."

His arm slipped around her waist and he hugged her tighter. He glanced over at Henrietta and Stan who were embracing each other for a job well-done. Indy and Pinky were talking to a grinning Fanny, and Jake was taking turns spinning the twins around in circles. "Let's get out of here for a minute. There's something I have to tell you."

"Can't it wait?" She relaxed in his embrace and smiled. She wanted to see her grandparents' expressions when the twins announced their news.

"It will only take a minute." He gently guided her out of the lounge and into the empty lobby. He backed her up until they were hidden by a forest of huge green plants. His fingers trembled as he stroked her soft cheek. "I missed you."

She pressed her cheek into the palm of his hand. "I'm still a great detective."

"I know." He brushed back a soft wisp of her hair and smiled at her look of astonishment. "That's what scared me."

"Scared you?"

"When I came here and was graciously going to *allow* you the victory, I was acting like a coward. I was really scared to death you would win and I would end up with egg all over my face." He kissed the end of her nose. "The Montgomerys are a formidable family to try to fit into. I figured the only way I could was to prove beyond a shadow of a doubt that I could hold my own against them."

"But, Reece, didn't you understand? We didn't want you against us. We wanted you with us." She reached up and cupped his cheek. "I never should have tried to outsmart you. I should have welcomed you into the family and graciously conceded defeat that first year."

"And last year?"

She very carefully straightened his tie. "I should have beaten the pants off you." She gave the knot a slight tug. "I would have, too, if you hadn't locked me in that basement. Right?"

Reece blanched as the knot tightened. "Absolutely, love." The knot slowly loosened. "You can match me any day of the week, Tennie. It doesn't frighten me anymore."

"Match—not beat?"

He laughed. "Match, you little minx, not beat." He kissed her soundly. "If I admit that you could beat me, you'd be impossible to live with." He kissed her a second time and succeeded to wipe the willful look off her face. "We are going to be equals, love. Take it or leave it."

"Equals, huh?" Tennie thought for a moment before wrapping her arms around his neck. "I like the sound of that." She raised her mouth and kissed him the way she had been dying to.

Heat exploded between them. He kissed the creamy smoothness of her neck. That enticing spot had been driving him crazy all night. "So have you picked a date yet?"

"For what?" Her fingers wove themselves into the silkiness of his hair.

"Our wedding."

Tennie froze. "What wedding?"

"The one we're going to announce in about five minutes."

"Why would we do that?"

"Because your family might take the idea of me carrying you up those steps and disappearing for the next week a whole lot easier if we gave them a date." He stroked away the apprehension from her lips with his thumb.

"But you don't want to marry me!"

He looked at her in surprise. "I don't?"

Tennie felt her heart begin to soar at the possibilities. "I can't cook."

He kissed the tip of her nose. "We'll eat out."

She bit her lip in concentration. "I'm not known for my housekeeping skills."

"We'll hire a housekeeper." He strung a line of kisses down her cheek and teased the corner of her mouth.

"I'll make a terrible mother."

"You'll make a wonderful mother." He nipped at her lower lip. "Are you by any chance trying to scare me off?"

She quickly said, "No! I mean, I don't want you to be disappointed. I want to keep working. I love being a detective. It's in the blood."

Reece saw the seriousness clouding the happiness in her eyes. Did she really think he'd ask her to change? "You can continue doing exactly what you have been doing, on one condition."

"What's that?"

"That I'm allowed to continue doing what I've been doing, Tennie." He cupped her chin and forced her to hold his gaze. "Don't you remember, love? We're equals." He kissed the smile forming on her lips. "In everything."

Tennie threw her arms around his neck. "Oh, Reece, I do love you!"

Reece swung her up into his arms and laughed. "You better"—he started to carry her toward the stairs—"considering what I plan on doing to you once we—"

"Reece! Tennie!" Indy cried.

Reece turned around and frowned at Indy. "Don't worry, it's the last Saturday in June."

Tennie was shocked and then surprised at Reece's comment. June was only two months away! Love was shining in Reece's eyes. She looked at her grandfather and grinned. "Yes, Pop-Pop, the last Saturday in June."

Indy looked confused for a moment before he shook his head. "I need your help."

"Can't it wait?" Reece begged.

"No, it can't wait. You two started it."

"Started what?" Tennie asked.

"North and South Carolina now think they're master detectives. They want to open up their own agency."

Reece felt Tennie's silent laughter. "What's wrong with that, sir?"

"They're going to use the name Montgomery!"

Reece bit down on his lower lip to keep the laughter in. Tennie couldn't meet her grandfather's gaze. "Their last name is Montgomery-Smyth."

"They're going to shorten it legally to Montgomery," Indy explained.

"So what do you want me and Reece to do about it?"

"Stop them! You're a Montgomery, Tennie. Don't you care what happens to that name?"

Tennie tightened her hold around Reece's neck and kissed his jaw. "Not particularly." Tennie knew that North and South Carolina had been asking for the family's financial support in opening up a fashion boutique in Carmel for years. So far no one had paid any attention to them. They were now doing what Tennie had advised them to do, scare the entire family into giving that support.

Indy's mouth fell open in astonishment.

"You see, Grandfather"—it was payback time for the matchmaking and scaring her half to death about Pinky's heart—"I'm about to become a Carpenter."

Reece couldn't stop kissing her as he carried her up the steps and down the hall to his room.

Indy stood at the bottom of the staircase, frowning. Tennie hated working with wood. So why would she want to become a carpenter? And what was that about the last Saturday in June? He jerked his shocked gaze from the empty steps as it finally hit him. Dear Lord! Reece and Tennie were getting married! He dashed back to the lounge, shouting, "Break out the champagne! We have a wedding to plan."

Pinky looked at Indy and grinned. "Oh good! Which wedding guest should we knock off this time?"

THE EDITOR'S CORNER

Summer is here at last, and we invite you to join us for our 11th anniversary. Things are really heating up with six wonderful new Loveswepts that sizzle with sexy heroes and dazzling heroines. As always, our romances are packed with tender emotion and steamy passion that are guaranteed to make this summer a hot one!

Always a favorite, Helen Mittermeyer gives us a heroine who is **MAGIC IN PASTEL**, Loveswept #690. When fashion model Pastel Marx gazes at Will Nordstrom, it's as if an earthquake hits him! Will desires her with an intensity that shocks him, but the anguish she tries to hide makes him want to protect her. Determined to help Pastel fight the demons that plague her, Will tries to comfort her, longing to know why his fairy-tale princess is imprisoned by her fear. Enveloped in the arms of a man whose touch soothes and arouses, Pastel struggles to accept the gift of his caring and keep their rare love true in a world of fire and ice. Helen delivers a story with characters that will warm your heart.

The heroine in Deborah Harmse's newest book finds herself **IN THE ARMS OF THE LAW,** Loveswept #691. Rebekah de Bieren decides Detective Mackenzie Hoyle has a handsome face, a great body, and a rotten attitude! When Mack asks Becky to help him persuade one of her students to testify in a murder case, he is stunned by this pint-sized blond angel who is as tempting as she is tough . . . but he refuses to take no for an answer—no matter how her blue eyes flash. Becky hears the sorrow behind Mack's cynical request and senses the tormented emotions he hides beneath his fierce dedication. Drawn to the fire she sees sparking in his cool gray eyes, she responds with shameless abandon—and makes him yearn for impossible dreams. Deborah Harmse will have you laughing and crying with this sexy romance.

FOR MEN ONLY, Loveswept #692, by the wonderfully talented Sally Goldenbaum, is a romance that cooks. The first time Ellie Livingston and Pete Webster met, he'd been a blind date from hell, but now he looks good enough to eat! Pete definitely has his doubts about taking a cooking class she's designed just for men, but his gaze is hungry for the pleasures only she can provide. Pete has learned not to trust beautiful women, but Ellie's smile is real—and full of temptation. Charmed by her spicy personality and passionate honesty, he revels in the sensual magic she weaves, but can Pete make her believe their love is enough? **FOR MEN ONLY** is a story you can really sink your teeth into.

Glenna McReynolds has given us another dark and dangerous hero in **THE DRAGON AND THE DOVE,** Loveswept #693. Cooper Daniels had asked for a female shark with an instinct for the jugular, but instead he's sent an angelfish in silk who looks too innocent to help him with his desperate quest to avenge his brother's death! Jessica Langston is fascinated by the hard sensuality of his face and mesmerized by eyes that meet hers with the force of a head-on collision, but she refuses to be dismissed—winning Cooper's respect and igniting his desire. Suddenly, Cooper is compelled by an inexorable need to claim her with tantalizing gentleness. Her surrender makes him yearn to rediscover the tenderness he's missed, but Cooper believes he'll only hurt the woman who has given him back his life. Jessica cherishes her tough hero, but now she must help heal the wounds that haunt his soul. **THE DRAGON AND THE DOVE** is Glenna at her heart-stopping best.

Donna Kauffman invites you to **TANGO IN PARADISE**, Loveswept #694. Jack Tango is devastatingly virile, outrageously seductive, and a definite danger to her peace of mind, but resort owner April Morgan needs his help enough to promise him whatever he wants—and she suspects what he wants is her in his arms! Jack wants her desperately but without regrets—and he'll wait until she pleads for his touch. April responds with wanton satisfaction to Jack's need to claim her soul, to possess and pleasure her, but even with him as her formidable ally, does she dare face old ghosts? **TANGO IN PARADISE** will show you why Donna is one of our brightest and fastest-rising stars.

Last, but definitely not least, is a battle of passion and will in Linda Wisdom's **O'HARA vs. WILDER**, Loveswept #695. For five years, Jake Wilder had been the man of her sexiest dreams, the best friend and partner she'd once dared to love, then leave, but seeing him again in the flesh leaves Tess O'Hara breathless . . . and wildly aroused! Capturing her mouth in a kiss that sears her to the toes and catches him in the fire-storm, Jake knows she is still more woman than any man can handle, but he is willing to try. Powerless to resist the kisses that brand her his forever, Tess fights the painful memories that their reckless past left her, but Jake insists they are a perfect team, in bed and out. Seduced by the electricity sizzling between them, tantalized beyond reason by Jake's wicked grin and rough edges, Tess wonders if a man who's always looked for trouble can settle for all she can give him. Linda Wisdom has another winner with **O'HARA vs. WILDER.**

Happy reading,

With warmest wishes,

Nita Taublib

Nita Taublib

Associate Publisher

P.S. Don't miss the women's novels coming your way in June—**WHERE SHADOWS GO,** by Eugenia Price, is an enthralling love story of the Old South that is the second volume of the *Georgia Trilogy,* following **BRIGHT CAPTIVITY; DARK JOURNEY,** by award-winning Sandra Canfield, is a heart-wrenching story of love and obsession, betrayal and forgiveness, in which a woman discovers the true price of forbidden passion; **SOMETHING BORROWED, SOMETHING BLUE,** by Jillian Karr, is a mixture of romance and suspense in which four brides—each with a dangerous secret—will be the focus of a deliciously glamorous issue of *Perfect Bride* magazine; and finally **THE MOON RIDER,** Virginia Lynn's most appealing historical romance to date, is a passionate tale of a highwayman and his lady-love. We'll be giving you a sneak peek at these wonderful books in next month's LOVESWEPTs. And immediately following this page look for a preview of the terrific romances from Bantam that are *available now!*

Don't miss these fantastic books by your
favorite Bantam authors

On sale in April:

DECEPTION
by *Amanda Quick*

RELENTLESS
by *Patricia Potter*

SEIZED BY LOVE
by *Susan Johnson*

WILD CHILD
by *Suzanne Forster*

Winner of *Romantic Times*
1992 Storyteller of the Year Award

Patricia Potter

Nationally Bestselling Author
Of **Notorious** and **Renegade**

RELENTLESS

*Beneath the outlaw's smoldering gaze, Shea Randall felt
a stab of pure panic . . . and a shiver of shocking desire.
Held against her will by the darkly handsome bandit,
she knew that for her father's sake she must find a
way to escape. Only later, as the days of her captivity
turned into weeks and Rafe Tyler's fiery passion sparked
her own, did Shea fully realize her perilous position—
locked in a mountain lair with a man who could steal
her heart . . .*

The door opened, and the bright light of the
afternoon sun almost blinded her. Her eyes were
drawn to the large figure in the doorway. Silhouetted by the sun behind him, Tyler seemed even
bigger, stronger, more menacing. She had to force
herself to keep from backing away.

He hesitated, his gaze raking over the cabin,
raking over her. He frowned at the candle.

She stood. It took all her bravery, but she stood,
forcing her eyes to meet his, to determine what was
there. There seemed to be nothing but a certain
coolness.

"I'm thirsty," she said. It came out as more of a challenge than a request, and she saw a quick flicker of something in his eyes. She hoped it was remorse, but that thought was quickly extinguished by his reply.

"Used to better places?" It was a sneer, plain and simple, and Shea felt anger stirring again.

"I'm used to gentlemen and simple . . . humanity."

"That's strange, considering your claim that you're Randall's daughter."

"I haven't claimed anything to you."

"That's right, you haven't," he agreed in a disagreeable voice. "You haven't said much at all."

"And I don't intend to. Not to a thief and a traitor."

"Be careful, Miss Randall. Your . . . continued health depends on this thief and traitor."

"That's supposed to comfort me?" Her tone was pure acid.

His gaze stabbed her. "You'll have to forgive me. I'm out of practice in trying to comfort anyone. Ten years out of practice."

"So you're going to starve me?"

"No," he said slowly. "I'm not going to do *that*."

The statement was ominous to Shea. "What are you going to do?"

"Follow my rules, and I won't do anything."

"You already are. You're keeping me here against my will."

He was silent for a moment, and Shea noted a muscle moving in his neck, as if he were just barely restraining himself.

"Lady, because of your . . . father, I was 'held'

against my will for ten years." She wanted to slap him for his mockery. She wanted to kick him where it would hurt the most. But now was not the time.

"Is that it? You're taking revenge out on me?"

The muscle in his cheek moved again. "No, Miss Randall, it's not that. You just happened to be in the wrong place at the wrong time. I don't have any more choices than you do." He didn't know why in the hell he was explaining, except her last charge galled him.

"You do."

He turned away from her. "Believe what you want," he said, his voice indifferent. "Blow out that candle and come with me if you want some water."

She didn't want to go with him, but she was desperate to shake her thirst. She blew out the candle, hoping that once outside he wouldn't see dried streaks of tears on her face. She didn't want to give him that satisfaction.

She didn't have to worry. He paid no attention to her, and she had to scurry to keep up with his long-legged strides. She knew she was plain, especially so in the loose-fitting britches and shirt she wore and with her hair in a braid. She also knew she should be grateful that he was indifferent to her, but a part of her wanted to goad him, confuse him . . . attract him.

Shea felt color flood her face. To restrain her train of thought, she concentrated on her surroundings.

Her horse was gone, although her belongings were propped against the tree stump. There was a shack to the left, and she noticed a lock on the door. That must be where he'd taken the weapons and where he kept his own horse. The keys must be in his pockets. He strode over to the building and picked up a bucket with his gloved hand.

She tried to pay attention to their route, but it seemed they had just melted into the woods and everything looked alike. She thought of turning around and running, but he was only a couple of feet ahead of her.

He stopped abruptly at a stream and leaned against a tree, watching her.

She had never drunk from a stream before, yet that was obviously what he expected her to do. The dryness in her mouth was worse, and she couldn't wait. She moved to the edge of the stream and kneeled, feeling awkward and self-conscious, knowing he was watching and judging. She scooped up a handful of water, then another, trying to sip it before it leaked through her fingers. She caught just enough to be tantalized.

She finally fell flat on her stomach and put her mouth in the water, taking long swallows of the icy cold water, mindless of the way the front of her shirt got soaked, mindless of anything but water.

It felt wonderful and tasted wonderful. When she was finally sated, she reluctantly sat up, and her gaze went to Tyler.

His stance was lazy but his eyes, like fine emeralds, were intense with fire. She felt a corresponding wave of heat consume her. She couldn't move her gaze from him, no matter how hard she tried. It was as if they were locked together.

He was the first to divert his gaze and his face settled quickly into its usual indifferent mask.

She looked down and noticed that her wet shirt clung to her, outlining her breasts. She swallowed hard and turned around. She splashed water on her face, hoping it would cool the heat suffusing her body.

She kept expecting Tyler to order her away, but he didn't. And she lingered as long as she could. She didn't want to go back to the dark cabin. She didn't want to face him, or those intense emotions she didn't understand.

She felt his gaze on her, and knew she should feel fear. He had been in prison a very long time. But she was certain he wouldn't touch her in a sexual way.

Because he despises you.

Because he despises your father.

She closed her eyes for a moment, and when she opened them, a spiral of light gleamed through the trees, hitting the stream. She wanted to reach out and catch that sunbeam, to climb it to some safe place.

But there were no safe places any longer.

She watched that ray of light until it slowly dissipated as the sun slipped lower in the sky, and then she turned around again. She hadn't expected such patience from Tyler.

"Ready?" he asked in his hoarse whisper.

The word held many meanings.

Ready for what? She wasn't ready for any of this.

But she nodded.

He sauntered over and offered his hand.

She refused it and rose by herself, stunned by how much she suddenly wanted to take his hand, to feel that strength again.

And Shea realized her battle wasn't entirely with him. It was also with herself.

"Susan Johnson brings sensuality to new heights and beyond."
—*Romantic Times*

SUSAN JOHNSON

Nationally bestselling author of **Outlaw** and **Silver Flame**

SEIZED BY LOVE

Now available in paperback

Sweeping from the fabulous country estates and hunting lodges to the opulent ballrooms and salons of the Russian nobility, here is a novel of savage passions and dangerous pleasures by the incomparable Susan Johnson, mistress of the erotic historical.

"*Under your protection?*" Alisa sputtered, flushing vividly as the obvious and unmistakable clarity of his explanation struck her. Of course, she should have realized. How very stupid of her. The full implication of what the public reaction to her situation would be left her momentarily stunned, devoured with shame. She was exceedingly thankful, for the first time since her parents' death, that they *weren't* alive to see the terrible depths to which she had fallen, the sordid fate outlined for her.

Irritated at the masterful certainty of Nikki's assumption, and resentful to be treated once more like a piece of property, she coldly said, "I don't recall placing myself under your protection."

"Come now, love," Nikki said reasonably, "if you recall, when I found you in that shed, your alternatives were surely limited; more severe beatings and possibly death if Forseus had continued drugging you. Hardly a choice of options, I should think. And consider it now," Nikki urged amiably, "plenty of advantages, especially if one has already shown a *decided* partiality for the man one has as protector. I'm not considered ungenerous, and if you contrive to please me in the future as well as you have to this date, we shall deal together quite easily."

Taking umbrage at his arrogant presumption that her role was to please *him*, Alisa indignantly said, "I haven't any *decided* partiality for you, you arrogant lecher, and furthermore—"

"Give me three minutes alone with you, my dear," Nikki interjected suavely, "and I feel sure I can restore my credit on that account."

Her eyes dropped shamefully before his candid regard, but she was angry enough to thrust aside the brief feeling of embarrassment, continuing belligerently. "Maria has some money of mine she brought with us. I'm not in *need* of protection."

"Not enough to buy you one decent gown, let alone support yourself, a child, and three servants," Nikki disagreed bluntly with his typical disregard for tact.

"Well, then," Alisa insisted heatedly, "I'm relatively well educated, young, and strong. I can obtain a position as governess."

"I agree in principle with your idea, but unfortunately, the pressures of existence in this world of travail serve to daunt the most optimistic hopes." His words were uttered in a lazy, mocking drawl. "For you, the role of governess"—the sarcasm in his voice was all too apparent—"is quite a pleasant conceit, my dear. You *will* forgive my speaking frankly, but I fear you are lacking in a sense of the realities of things.

"*If*—I say, *if*—any wife in her right mind would allow a provokingly beautiful young woman like yourself to enter her household, I'd wager a small fortune, the master of that house would be sharing your bed within the week. Consider the folly of the notion, love. At least with me there'd be no indignant wife to throw you and your retinue out into the street when her husband's preferences became obvious. And since I have a rather intimate knowledge of many of these wives, I think my opinion is to be relied upon. And as your protector," he continued equably, "I, of course, feel an obligation to maintain your daughter and servants in luxurious comfort."

"I am not a plaything to be bought!" Alisa said feelingly.

"Ah, my dear, but you are. Confess, it is a woman's role, primarily a pretty plaything for a man's pleasure and then inexorably as night follows day— a mother. Those are the two roles a woman plays. It's preordained. Don't fight it," he said practically.

Alisa would have done anything, she felt at that moment, to wipe that detestable look of smugness from Nikki's face.

"Perhaps I'll take Cernov up on his offer after all," she said with the obvious intent to provoke. "Is he richer than you? I must weigh the advantages if

I'm to make my way profitably in the demimonde," she went on calculatingly. "Since I'm merely a play-thing, it behooves me to turn a practical frame of mind to the role of demirep and sell myself for the highest price in money and rank obtainable. I have a certain refinement of background—"

"Desist in the cataloguing if you please," he broke in rudely, and in a dangerously cold voice murmured, "Let us not cavil over trifles. You're staying with me." Alisa involuntarily quailed before the stark, open challenge in his eyes, and her heart sank in a most unpleasant way.

"So my life is a trifle?" she whispered, trembling with a quiet inner violence.

"You misunderstand, my dear," the even voice explained with just a touch of impatience. "It's sim-ply that I don't intend to enter into any senseless wrangles or debates over your attributes and the direction in which your favors are to be bestowed. Madame, you're to remain my mistress." His lips smiled faintly but the smile never reached his eyes.

WILD CHILD
by Suzanne Forster
bestselling author of
SHAMELESS

"A storyteller of incandescent brilliance . . . beyond compare in a class by herself . . . that rare talent, a powerhouse writer whose extraordinary sensual touch can mesmerize . . ."
—*Romantic Times*

Her memorable characters and sizzling tales of romance and adventure have won her numerous awards and countless devoted readers. Now, with her trademark blend of intense sensuality and deep emotion, Suzanne Forster reunites adversaries who share a tangled past— and for whom an old spark of conflict will kindle into a dangerously passionate blaze . . .

"I want to talk about us," he said.
"Us?"
Blake could have predicted the stab of panic in her eyes, but he couldn't have predicted what was happening inside Cat. As she met his gaze, she felt herself dropping, a wind-rider caught in a powerful downdrift. The plummeting sensation in her stomach was sudden and sharp. The dock seemed to go out from under her feet, and as she imagined herself falling, she caught a glimpse of something in her mind that riveted her.
Surrender.
Even the glimpse of such naked emotion was terrifying to Cat. It entranced and enthralled her. It

was the source of her panic. It was the wellspring of her deepest need. To be touched, to be loved. She shuddered in silence and raised her face to his.

By the time he did touch her, the shuddering was deep inside her. It was emotional and sexual and beautiful. No, she thought, this is impossible. This isn't happening. *Not with this man. Not with him . . .*

He curved his hand to her throat and drew her to him.

"What do I do, Cat?" he asked. "How do I make the sadness go away?"

The question rocked her softly, reverberating in the echo chamber her senses had become. *Not this man. Not him. He's hurt you too much. . . .*

"Sweet, sad, Cat." He caressed the underside of her chin with long, long strokes of his thumb. The sensations were soft and erotic and thrilling, and they accomplished exactly what they were supposed to, Cat realized, bringing her head up sharply. He wanted her to look up at him. He wanted her throat arched, her head tilted back.

No, Cat! He's hurt you too much.

"Don't," she whispered. "Not you . . ."

"Yes, Cat, me," he said. "It has to be me."

He bent toward her, and his lips touched hers with a lightning stroke of tenderness. Cat swallowed the moan in her throat. In all her guilty dreams of kissing Blake Wheeler—and there had been many—she had never imagined it as tender. She never had imagined a sweetness so sharp that it would fill her throat and tear through her heart like a poignant memory. Was this how lovers kissed? Lovers who had hurt each other and now needed to be very, very cautious? Lovers whose wounds weren't healed?

Age-old warnings stirred inside her. She should have resisted, she wanted to resist, but as his lips brushed over hers she felt yearnings flare up inside her—a wrenchingly sweet need to deepen the kiss, to be held and crushed in his arms. She had imagined him as self-absorbed, an egotistical lover who would take what he wanted and assume that being with him was enough for any woman. A night with Blake Wheeler. A night in heaven! She had imagined herself rejecting him, ordering him out of her bed and out of her life. She had imagined all of those things so many times . . . but never *tenderness*.

His mouth was warm. It was as vibrant as the water sparkling around them. She touched his arm, perhaps to push him away, and then his lips drifted over hers, and her touch became a caress. Her fingers shimmered over heat and muscle, and she felt a sudden, sharp need to be closer.

All of her attention was focused on the extraordinary thing that was happening to her. A kiss, she told herself, *it was just a kiss*. But he touched her with such rare tenderness. His fingers plucked at her nerve-strings as if she were a delicate musical instrument. His mouth transfused her with fire and drained her of energy at the same time. And when at last his arms came around her and brought her up against him, she felt a sweet burst of physical longing that saturated her senses.

She had dreamt of his body, too. And the feel of him now was almost more reality than she could stand. His thighs were steel, and his pelvic bones dug into her flesh. He was hard, righteously hard, and even the slightest shifts in pressure put her in touch with her own keening emptiness.

His tongue stroked her lips, and she opened

them to him slowly, irresistibly. On some level she knew she was playing a sword dance with her own emotions, tempting fate, tempting heartbreak, but the sensations were so exquisite, she couldn't stop herself. They seemed as inevitable and sensual as the deep currents swaying beneath them.

The first gliding touch of his tongue against hers electrified her. A gasp welled in her throat as he grazed her teeth and tingled sensitive surfaces. The penetration was deliciously languid and deep. By the time he lifted his mouth from hers, she was shocked and reeling from the taste of him.

The urge to push him away was instinctive.

"No, Cat," he said softly, inexplicably, "it's mine now. The sadness inside you is mine."

Studying her face, searching her eyes for something, he smoothed her hair and murmured melting suggestions that she couldn't consciously decipher. They tugged at her sweetly, hotly, pulling her insides to and fro, eliciting yearnings. Cat's first awareness of them was a kind of vague astonishment. It was deep and thrilling, what was happening inside her, like eddying water, like the sucking and pulling of currents. She'd never known such oddly captivating sensations.

The wooden dock creaked and the bay swelled gently beneath them, tugging at the pilings. Cat sighed as the rhythms of the sea and the man worked their enchantment. His hands *were* telepathic. They sought out all her tender spots. His fingers moved in concert with the deep currents, stroking the sideswells of her breasts, arousing her nerves to rivulets of excitement.

"Wild," he murmured as he cupped her breasts in his palms. "Wild, wild child."

And don't miss these spectacular
romances from Bantam Books,
on sale in May:

DARK JOURNEY
by the bestselling author
Sandra Canfield
"(Ms. Canfield's) superb style of writing
proves her to be an author extraordinaire."
—*Affaire de Coeur*

SOMETHING BORROWED
SOMETHING BLUE
by
Jillian Karr
"Author Jillian Karr . . . explodes onto the
mainstream fiction scene . . . Great reading."
—*Romantic Times*

THE MOON RIDER
by the highly acclaimed
Virginia Lynn
"A master storyteller."
—*Rendezvous*